I0779645

For my mother, thank you for helping me find my

way to live my dream.

DARK ANGEL

MELANIE CRIM

Trigger Warnings:

Possessiveness, Degradation, CNC, Child abuse, Rape, Bondage, Torture, Kidnapping, Breath Play, Orgasm withholding, Suicide, Stalking, Blood, Biting, Marking, Drug use, murder, and Castration.

Please take these seriously.

If any of this offends you, then please don't move forward with reading my story. This is a complete work of fiction for entertainment purposes only. I do not condone this type of relationship by any means.

Lincoln Hamilton Reynolds III is a very, very bad dude. Thankfully, he only lives in my head.

But this story is for anyone who loves a great villain and 'happy ever after'.

Enjoy!

PLAYLIST

99 Problems – Jay Z

The Wretched – NIN

Vicarious – Tool

We're In This Together – NIN

jealousy, jealousy – Olivia Rodrigo

Even Deeper – NIN

Woman of the Hour – Stela Cole

Blackout – Freya Ridings

Nails – Call Me Karizma

Ending Credits

Graveyard – Halsey

A villain's love is the truest form of love.

For a villain knows no love, other than true love.

PROLOGUE

I am running through an unfamiliar house in an intensive effort to escape. Every door I come to in this long, dark hallway is locked. I desperately need to cross the threshold of one of them.

Any of them.

I don't care.

My heart feels like it could jump out of my chest. I swore I could feel *him* gaining on me with every short breath that I took running through the huge house. Suddenly, my wrist twists, and I open the door to my potential exit. I rush inside, slam the door behind me, and lock it.

Shit.

I probably could have closed that a little softer.

I listen as I try to slow down my beating heart.

Silence.

Maybe I lost him, or whoever it was.

I move my shaky hand towards the wall next to me, looking for a light switch. I find one and flip it up. I see that this door didn't lead me to an exit. Instead, I am in a very large bathroom. There are two toilets to the right of me and I notice one is a bidet. The large, glass doored shower to my left has three heads. The sink is directly across from me, showcasing a long, wide mirror. I see my reflection and give myself a much-needed breath.

Fuck.

No windows.

I am stuck.

I lean back on the door, close my eyes, and take a few deep breaths. In through the nose and slowly out the mouth, count 1...2...3...4.

I can hear the bass of the music coming from downstairs, but other than that, there is nothing. Just the sounds of my frantic breaths going in and out of my buzzed body. As soon as my nervous system realized we could abandon the 'fight or flight' response, I started to feel less panicky.

What the fuck happened?

Lincoln.

I hadn't felt him so powerfully since I moved here about 4 months ago. But this was the first time I fully let my guard down. I didn't expect Jacob to make a move on me like he did. As soon as I rejected him, I thought I saw someone move quickly towards me from the corner of my eye. That shadow gave me a drop in my stomach, and the small hairs on the back of my neck stood. I felt like a serial killer had found me hidden in a small closet. My body just took over, and it led me here.

I need to calm my shit down. I reach into the pocket of my black dress and pop in the last Xanax. It's going to have to do till I get home. Out of habit, I rub my emerald heart necklace between my thumb and forefinger.

I shakily walk to the long, white granite sink and turn the faucet. The cold liquid drips through my fingers, and it relieves my hot skin. I cup a handful, bring it to my mouth, and throw the coolness back down my throat. I just need to wait a little bit till this kicks in.

I plop my black, dainty purse on the counter to pull out my ChapStick and reapply. I wondered if Michelle was looking for me by now. Granted, my roommate was probably wasted at this point. We had pre-gamed before we came to this party, and she was a light weight on a normal day. Honestly, I was surprised to meet a nineteen-year-old who had never tried vodka before. I had my first sip of vodka at 11 years old, given to me by my alcoholic mother. She wanted to see if it would make me more fun to be around.

It didn't.

I ended up puking my guts out the remainder of the night after she had forced me to take two shots. I was so scared I had alcohol poisoning, but she slapped me across the face saying that I was a naive little shit. The memory of that night just reiterated to me why I needed to keep my past my past.

I wanted to keep an eye on Michelle tonight, but Jacob asked me to follow him outside to sit by the pool. I could tell he had been drinking, too, because he smelled like a brewery. I left Michelle in the kitchen, telling her I would just be outside.

It felt like a mistake when he held my hand and led me out to the lounge chairs. There were lots of people crowded around us, talking and drinking. I allowed him to sit close to me even though I felt claustrophobic.

I knew he had a crush on me based on the number of times he had asked me out on dates. I declined him politely every time, but he still pursued me. He reminded me too much of Nick, and I didn't need another 'brother' in my life. I hadn't talked with Nick in over 7 months, and it was better that way.

The one person who could have me begging on my bruised knees for a single touch wasn't here. I ran from Lincoln because I didn't belong in his world. I belonged here, in this one.

Here, I had a job, I made some friends, I was planning to go to college in the fall, and I was finally going to start a new life. But, with a new life, I had to make some compromises. One of those being Michelle.

Michelle is relentless when it comes to something she wants. All week, she had been begging me to let her dress me for tonight. But the final nail in the coffin was when she offered to cover groceries for a month. That was a dealbreaker. She put me in a strapless black dress that fit like it was tailor-made for me.

It was tightly fitted around my decent B-sized breasts. Although, I think the built in bra made them look slightly bigger. The soft fabric flared out from my hips and reached just above my knees. I regretted the black strapped heels the moment we stepped onto the street. God, they were really killing me now. She also insisted on doing my makeup. She did what she called a 'smoky eye' around my green ones followed by heavy mascara.

When I moved here, I needed a new identity in case Lincoln started to look for me. I dyed my hair back to its natural dark-brown-mahogany color and started going by my middle name, Rose. My head was throbbing now, so I relieved the pain by letting down my ponytail. I used my fingers and fluffed out my long, wavy locks.

Knock, knock!

The loud noise startles me half to death. I feel like my heart is about to beat out of my chest for the second time tonight.

"Just a minute," I yell to whoever is on the other side.

KNOCK! KNOCK!

I jump again from the aggressiveness. It sounded like the door could've come off the hinges. I huff and grab my purse while stomping towards the door. "Alright, alright...hold your hors-"

I open the door, and my voice is cut off by those dark blue eyes staring back at me.

No, no, no....it can't be.

The door, which I forgot was still in my hand, is forcefully pulled out of my grasp. Lincoln's strong arm comes out and pushes it till it hits the wall. I stumble back until my tailbone hit the marble countertop of the sink. The pain doesn't even register. I can't catch my breath. My heart rate is increasing, and my chest tightens painfully with each inhale. My hands are sweaty, and I must have lost my voice.

I can't speak. My tongue weighs heavy inside my dry mouth.

My mind can't think...it's a dream. It's a nightmare...it can't be real.

Lincoln is not standing in front of me right now with that sinister dark hair. I close my eyes, hoping that he is just a hallucination. My mind is just playing tricks on me again. But when I open them, I see him standing there. He's not an illusion. He is very real.

Very fucking real.

He strolls into the bathroom as if he has all the time in the world. His heavy steel-toed boots beat on the tile like thunder during a storm. His designer blue jeans are being held up by a large black belt. Instinctively, I smell the leather, and my wrists start to ache as if they were conditioned. I remember the feel of that leather against my wrists, and my pussy clenches.

He wears a black zippered hoodie underneath a ripped denim jacket. The hoodie is open revealing a white t-shirt. His shirt is covered in blood.

His blue eyes stare back at me intently.

He doesn't look angry, but he doesn't look pleased to see me either. He looks emotionless, and I don't know why, but that scares me more than if he were furious. How long has he known where to find me?

Lincoln never breaks eye contact as he eerily closes the door slowly.

The click of the lock is deafening in this quiet room.

I try to swallow, but nothing comes.

Lincoln walks to the center of the room and stops. He slowly puts his hands in the front pockets of his jeans and lets out a deep breath through his flared nostrils. His hair looks the same as it did all those months ago when I saw him last. It's a dark, chocolate-brown mess hanging low on his forehead. He glances down at the floor and runs up my body leisurely, making me feel naked. I want to hug myself with my arms to provide some level of comfort. But I can't. They weigh heavy and useless by my sides. My feet have cemented into the floor.

My nipples are painfully aware of themselves, but I remind them that this is Lincoln. He told me many times that no one fucked with what was his, and he made me *his* a long time ago. I was only deceiving myself, thinking I could run from him. I will never be able to get away. He has claimed me from the inside out.

Not even my own soul belongs to me now.

I patiently wait for his eyes to settle on mine and silently wait for his commands. And damn, this scene looks awfully familiar. Reminding me of the first time we were together.

His gaze finally reaches my eyes. A sly smile spreads across his handsome face.

"Did you miss me, baby?" he muses, indicating that he also recognizes the similarities of this scene.

My body betrays me like she does every fucking time he opens his mouth. His deep voice sends shivers throughout my entire body. My clit calls for my attention, allowing my arousal to flow out. I hate how he has this effect on me. My body craves the depravity that is Lincoln Hamilton Reynolds III.

"Why can't you just let me go, Link?" I desperately ask.

The adrenaline I have is fading fast, and the Xanax is suddenly kicking in. I feel like I can barely keep my body standing up anymore.

"Awe, baby," he advances towards me until we are toe-to-toe. His six-foot, lean frame towers over me.

I strain my neck, looking up at his dominating figure. I am more afraid of what will happen if I look away than looking into those deep blue, dark depths that swallow me whole. They have no remorse for what they cause inside of me. They will make me beg for the ticket to hell with a lustful smile on my greedy, cum-stained face.

His left hand comes up to rest on the hair at the back of my skull. He grabs a fistful. I cry out in pain and pleasure. His grip easily expresses to me his state of mind.

He is fucking livid with me.

He pulls my head back, so I have to look at the ceiling above us. His tight grip and domination are unnerving. I want to grab onto his shirt. I want to pull him into me. I want to wrap my legs around him and have him rub his hard cock against my center.

Yes, in this moment, he is my God.

And I am his unworthy slave.

I should have known better...I shouldn't have run from him. He knew what I always wanted because he was fully aware of all my fucked-up kinks.

I feel his other hand close around my jaw tightly. His touch is painful, but I know he's holding back. I feel the wetness pool in my panties. My cunt expects more pain with her pleasure and greedily anticipates every moment to come. And yes, she fully intended that pun because she is a fucking traitor. She always betrays me when it comes to him.

He pinches my jaw more while his gorgeous smirk widens across his face. A taste of copper populates on my cheeks from the intense pressure. I try to move my head to the side, but he maintains all the control I thought I had.

He tilts my head to the side.

I feel the wetness of Lincoln's tongue as he slowly licks up the tear I didn't feel falling down my right cheek.

"Always so fucking beautiful, Allie."

My hot insides finally melt at the sound of my first name falling from his soft lips. My pussy weeps into the seams of my panties polluting the air with her distinctive salty, sweet scent. Her God has rescued her from this extensive dry spell and she thanks him the only way she knows how to; aromatically.

The warmth from my center causes more tears to fall from my eyes. "Fuck," I sigh out wishing I didn't want him so badly.

His forehead drops to meet mine, and his eyes close. I feel his breath on my face and a light kiss from his lips as he whispers, "Welcome home, baby."

As soon as his words leave his lips, it's like the flash of a camera going off. All my hopes for this new place and my dreams for the next year suddenly vanish.

I close my eyes and see Michelle waving goodbye. I see Jacob wondering why I never got back to him about going to the park next weekend. I see my coworkers wondering what happened to Rose, the name by which they all know me.

All of it catches fire, and all that remains is ash and the lingering smoke.

But then, out of the ashes like a phoenix rising, I see a figure approach. Who do I see approaching me from that thick coat of soot?

Lincoln Hamilton Reynolds III.

His strong arms wrap around me, crushing my lungs, taking my breath, and never letting me go.

"Mine."

His voice brings me out of my daydream and back into reality. I open my eyes and feel a wet cloth on my mouth. He holds me tight as I struggle to get free. I inhale and exhale, but it's too much. I feel my arms and legs slowly losing this battle. My head gets fuzzy.

"Shhh, shh, baby. Don't worry. It's ok. Everything is going to be ok. We're going home."

I blink my heavy eyelids and feel my body go limp in Lincoln's possessive arms.

"I got you now," he whispers in my ear, and then everything goes black.

It's all over now.

Lincoln Hamilton Reynolds III

"Kneel."

I command the big, busty blonde standing in the middle of our Billard's room in the basement. She's wearing a black G-string that comes up high on her narrow hips. She sways a bit unsteadily on her high heels. I assume she wears those, thinking they will make her less-than-average-looking legs look sexier, but it does nothing for me. I need her to be crying, screaming, begging, or chocking on my hard cock to get anywhere these days.

However, I feel like I want to play with this one for a bit, so let's see what she can do. "Crawl to me and kiss my boot."

I take another gulp of my watered-down McCallan and wait for her to get going. Her sloppy movements indicate she had too much to drink and finally got the nerve to hit on me. It's the same fucking thing I see every fucking time I throw a party. Bitches want to put a collar on me once they know who I am and what I can do for them. I am the son of a Senator, and my family owns the largest construction company on the East Coast. My grandfather started Reynolds Construction in his late teens. Therefore, most of the buildings that surround our town were built by us. All of the buildings in our town were built by us. We own it all.

But I digress.

This girl caught my eye when she wandered over and put her hand on my leg. She leaned in and asked me if I wanted to go somewhere to 'talk'. I knew then she wanted to fuck. I'll get this one to suck my dick instead of fucking her. I don't fuck drunk girls. There is no fun if they don't remember all the fucked up things I did to them the night before.

Another annoyance about this one is that she's hesitant, which I can enjoy on occasion, but tonight isn't the night to be coy. I need to shove my cock into her willing or unwilling mouth soon.

I drag my hand down my face and sigh, thinking about this entire fucked up day. Since meeting with my father earlier, I have been fucking pissed. This pounding in the front of my skull won't go away, and I'm antsy as fuck.

Before my father left to catch his flight out of the country, he told me to be prepared for my first assignment when he got back. He wouldn't give me any more details than that. He may think my crew and I don't know what the fuck we are doing, but he also has no idea. Derek and I have been working on a few things I wanted to share with him today, but he had other plans. He cut me off every time.

Fuck him.

If he doesn't want to hear about how we were able to find, execute, and hide the dumb motherfucker who stole from us three months ago, then fuck him. I tighten my hand around the glass and feel it on the brink of shattering.

Just as I am about to tell this bitch to start sucking or grabbing her shit to leave, Derek busts into the room. His hair is a mess, and he continues to button up his jeans.

"We got a problem, Link…. looks like someone is in the main room trying to cut off Brett Johnson's balls." He smiles, knowing how much I would love to see some violence and bloodshed tonight.

I finish the rest of my drink and place it on the crystal-clear coffee table in front of me. I jump up from my spot on the couch and tell the blonde not to go anywhere. She may come in handy once I get to purge some of this energy out of my body.

I walk up the stairs, down the hall into the main living area, off the left side of the house, and past the kitchen. Everyone seems to have stopped partying, but the music is still blaring through the house. Jay-Z is talking about having 99 problems, but it looks like people stopped to watch the show as much as I did…nice…I love an audience. As I round the corner, I hear her voice before I get a chance to see who is providing all this fun in my home.

"Get the fuck off of me, you fucking dickhead! I am here for Brett, and that motherfucker better show himself. Brett! Brett! Where the fuck are you, asshole?"

One of my main soldiers, Tyler, who stands at 6 foot 4 and is all muscle, is holding onto a fierce little thing. Dressed in all black from head to toe, she tries to fight, claw, and bite with all that she has, but she isn't going anywhere. Tyler holds onto this girl like she is a feral kitten he picked up off the dirty streets. She's tenacious, but it's no match against his size.

"Where the fuck is he? That fucking coward better show himself, or I am not leaving till he does. Brett! Brett! Where the fuck are you?" She yells, throwing her head back and forth from side to side. She yells and kicks Tyler while he holds both sides of her arms down.

Tyler looks over at me, silently asking what I want him to do with her. I give my head a downward nod, letting him know to keep her captive. I want her to tire out a little more before we let her go, and who knows, maybe this Brett pussy will show his face aft-.

Oh, and speak of the mother fucking devil...

"What the fuck is this little cunt doing here? Doesn't she know we don't allow skanks on this side of the tracks?" Brett spits out, giving his buddy a high five and laughing. I want to vomit at his juvenile behavior.

His antics encourage a little crowd behind him as he attempts to taunt my little troublemaker. *I* feel like cutting off his balls.

I get ready to tell him to fuck off, but suddenly, this girl forcefully crashes her boot onto Tyler's shin, causing him to let her go. She whips out of his grasp and goes straight for Brett.

The sneaky little thing gets to him before his meek posse pulls her off. Fortunately for me, they don't get to her in time before she stabs him with a pocket knife in his throwing arm. Blood comes gushing out, and Brett, being the pussy that we know he is, starts to scream like a little girl.

Pathetic.

I am reveling in the scene before me. It's fucking perfect and just what I needed tonight.

Tyler recovers quickly and is able to grab her before she rams into Brett again. Some cheerleaders have started to tend to his needs, and the girl who steals my attention is still yelling profanities his way.

Derek kicks the pocketknife the little kitten dropped under the couch for us to grab later. I am never above blackmailing anyone. Derek is smart. His family is powerful, but not as much as mine is. His parents' law firm is one of the most prominent ones in the country. Our families knew each other in college, so we ended up growing up together. He is popular with the ladies as they refer to him as a 'fuckboy'. And he is pretty much the definition of that.

Tyler stands the girl up to me so I can get a better look at her. He holds her tight, and she finally turns to look at me.

Fuck.

Me.

And all that is unholy.

If I had a heart, it would stop.

This girl before me has blood spattered all over her pale skin. Her blonde hair is fucked all different ways, but I can see its not her natural. She has darker hair below the blonde strands. Her eyes are the color of a deep, dark forest. She is fucking gorgeous.

The blood of her enemy remains on her face, looking like the red freckles she was born with.

Did the devil send you to me? I can't help the smile that spreads across my face. I feel like a kid on Christmas morning.

Her breathing is heavy as strands of her hair fly up and down on her face. She glares at me with a look of defiance.

Fuck.

Me.

Again.

And that, ladies and gentlemen, is when my dick decides to make an appearance all by himself for the first time in weeks.

Yes. This fucking girl is mine.

Thank you, Satan. I owe you big time.

I nudge my head towards the front door, telling Tyler to take her outside. She continues to glare at me while still yelling over her shoulder how she is coming back to finish what she started. Her body wiggles, and she tries to break free again from Tyler's hold, but she won't get away from him. He is a soldier...and true soldiers learn from their mistakes.

I was in elementary school when I found Tyler beating up a group of kids from our class in the yard. That's when I knew he would be a great service to me. His family lives in our gated community, but they are in the entertainment business. He is the tall, dark, strong, silent type with a military-style haircut.

Once we step outside, Tyler lets go of the irate little kitten and then comes to stand on my left. Derek follows to stand on my right. I wait till she has settled down with all her huffing and puffing before I think of what to do with her.

Damn, she is on fire.

Once she regains her breathing and the adrenaline appears to be leaving her body, I motion to the guys to head inside.

I stand in front of her small frame and wonder what her body must look like under that oversized hoodie. She wears black boots and black skintight leggings with holes in the knees. God, I would love to sink my sharp canines into those thick thighs and draw blood. I would listen to her scream my na—

"What are you going to do now...call the cops on me?" She spits, pushing the strands of her hair behind her ears and cutting off my trail of preferred thoughts.

Her ignorance is adorable.

I smile and wonder how much this girl really knows about me. The look in her eyes was still burning with a vengeance. I know little one...I know that feeling. Soon, you can purge, maybe even with me.

And now my dick is even harder.

I chuckled out loud to ease her worry.

"No. No cops get called to this house. And if they did, they would ignore it unless it came directly from me, and I have no intention of calling them."

I lean against the brick and pull a cigarette from the soft pack in my pocket. I watch my little toy figure out her next play because I am all for playing.

Come on, little one...play with me.

Allie

Fuck me...I knew that coming here tonight was a gamble. I knew that I could possibly run into Lincoln Reynolds himself, but I did not think I would catch his attention this much. I am truly fucked, but I need to figure out how to get out of this. He leans against this huge fucking house and doesn't seem to care that people continue to come in and out as he stands here pulling out a Parliament to smoke.

His tall, slender frame is intimidating, but not as much as his aura. He doesn't even have to say anything for me to feel his presence all over my body. He has striking blue eyes and dark hair. It's all messed up as if he just rolled out of bed, or had some girl rub her manicured hands all through it, and yet it's perfect. It hangs just over his eyes in a beautiful mess on his pretty head.

God, his face is straight out of a Paris fashion runway show. Not that I have ever seen one, but I can make my assumptions, for goodness' sake. I see his long jawbone and notice his adam's apple bob up and down as he swallows. God damn, I didn't know those could be so sexy.

Every time he smiles, my panties get wet. And this is not the time for that...what the fuck was I thinking?

This was all wrong. And now, I just cut up the throwing arm that belongs to Yaverson College's football quarterback.

I am totally fucked.

He will press charges.

I will go to jail.

Everyone there saw me...he has tons of witnesses, and did I mention that my life is officially fucked. Why did I have to let my temper get the best of me...why did I use Brett as an excuse not to put a knife to who I really wish I could? And why does Lincoln Reynolds have to look so goddamn tempting?

God, I hate my body reacting to shit that it shouldn't. Bad body! Bad body!

He pulls out a black zippo from his front pocket to light his cigarette. He inhales deeply and lets it out into the cool night air. I wore Nick's hoodie tonight because I knew I was planning on doing this shit, and I didn't want to get any evidence on my clothes.

Evidence...fuck.

I almost roll my eyes towards myself, but I get caught in those dark pools staring back at me.

I had heard stories from other girls about how attractive he was, but I didn't know that part of that appeal was just being around him. He makes me feel lightheaded and giddy inside.

I feel like I am not even wearing clothes at the moment, and I also feel like someone could come up behind me to slit my throat at any given moment. That is strangely disturbing and turning me on at the same time. What is wrong with me?

He pulls another drag from his cigarette, squinting his eyes. The glow cascading down his face from the porch light above his head makes him look mysterious. Lincoln exhibits a confidence that intimidates me to my core. His allure is intensified by the I-don't-give-a-fuck attitude. God, he is sexy.

"What's your name?" Lincoln asks, pulling me out of my own thoughts.

Fuck...I shouldn't give him my real name, right? An alias. Yep.

"Taylor," I yell out in a rush and purse my lips together. Damn, that didn't sound fake.

He cocks his eyebrow and asks me, "Is that what Brett would say as well if I ask him?"

Damn it.

Well, didn't think of that one now, did you, Allie?

Stupid.

Remind yourself never to commit another crime without thinking through all types of questions you may be asked. I shoot him a defeated smile, give a small sigh, and state the bold truth.

"Allie. My name is Allie Parker, if you must know. There!" I say, slapping my hands to my sides. "That way, you can tell anyone you want who came into your house and fucked up your party. Spilled blood all over your expensive carpets. And now the entire football season is ruined. Ok!" I end with a huff.

I give up...fuck my life after high school. Fuck my plans for college. My mother will just have another reason to mention why I was a mistake and a disappointment.

A few moments pass while I wait for the judgment to come.

Why is he just staring as my world collapses inside my head? I think maybe I should just turn around and run, but then he...smiles.

"You know what, come back inside," he states as he pushes himself off the brick wall. "I am sure you can see how much you did not fuck up anything. In fact, you threatening to cut off Brett Johnson's balls is, by far, my most favorite part of this day. The only reason I may be upset is because it had to happen at my house in front of all those witnesses. Trust me...if we were anywhere else but my father's house, I wouldn't have stopped you. Hell, I would have loved to join you." He exhales the smoke from his lungs.

He flicks the last bit of his cigarette off his thumb with his middle finger. It flies into the yard like an orange lightning bug. He starts to head back inside. Assuming that I will follow, but instead, I just stand there. Frozen.

No, I can't go back inside. He just stated the act of violence would not have mattered to him one bit and that he would have participated. He looks back over his shoulder, frowning.

"What's the problem?" He questions me.

"I can't go back inside...sorry, but I, um, I need to get back home. I shouldn't have come, and it was out of character for me, honestly. I am so sorry to have disturbed your party again. If I could just maybe use your phone for a minute to call my friend to come get me, I can be out of your hair."

My word vomit is admirable.

Lincoln just stands there inquisitively, and I feel heat radiating off my body. If I were a space heater, I could likely heat my entire trailer in five minutes.

My guess is he doesn't hear the word 'no' very often. So maybe the fact I was telling him that now was the reason for his standoffishness. I knew his father was a Senator, so he probably got away with things like murder. I laugh internally. But that didn't seem to discourage me from coming over here and stabbing a motherfucker.

After hearing what that pussy Brett did to Stephanie...I couldn't stand it. I had to do something because I knew nothing would happen to Brett. He would get off fucking free, and I was tired of seeing assholes like him go free.

"I'll give you a ride," he breaks the silence with this resolution to my problem.

He suddenly knocks on the front door twice, and it opens as if it is programmed.

A tall, blonde-haired boy pops out, holding a red solo cup. "Hey, what's up?" He asks Lincoln.

Lincoln whispers in blondie's ear, and he nods, never giving me the time of day. He closes the door, and Lincoln proceeds to walk past me down the numerous steps below us. I catch his scent as he walks by me: Besides the cigarette smell, he smells floral, like a bouquet of freshly bloomed lilies.

I try to catch up to him since he is significantly taller than me. His blue jeans hang off his hips, and I can't help but stare at his ass. It looks really nice, and I never check out asses on guys. His black t-shirt fits him so well over his lean but muscular body.

Lincoln approaches a fancy-looking sports car, and at this moment, I am reminded of his family. They are rich, and I don't mean just a little rich — I mean filthy rich.

The world I come from is the polar opposite. My life is hard and pitiful. I live with my mom in a small, dirty, double-wide trailer and walk to school every day. It sucks, but I know I only have a few more months, and then I can leave. I need to get my diploma so I can get the hell out of this town and start fresh somewhere else. Somewhere where no one knows me or my past.

"Hop in," his voice brings me back to the present.

The doors to Lincoln's sports car flip straight up in the air and startle the fuck out of me. I let out a sequel, and as soon as it leaves my mouth, I hear a deep chuckle. I look down to see he is already sitting and waiting for me to get in.

I don't know what was so funny...this rich prick didn't know anything about me. But instead of causing a scene with him, I let him have this one. After all, I did just stab someone in his living room minutes ago, and he bluntly indicated he would have loved to see more. I shouldn't push my luck.

I take a moment to think if I should get in the car with him at all. But my options are limited so I decide to take a chance. I have to get back home somehow.

Once I sit on the leather seat, the door descends. I feel like I have just entered a spaceship. When Lincoln turns over the engine, I definitely feel like I'm in a spaceship. This fancy thing is loud, and my body jiggles from the rumble of the engine. NIN's 'The Wretched' starts up on the sound system.

"Put in your address on my phone." He hands me the latest model iPhone, and I meekly ask for his password.

"I don't have one."

"What? You don't have a passcode for your phone?" I ask, dumbfounded.

He shrugs and gets settled more into his seat. He places his forearm over the wheel and stares out the windshield. "Don't need to. No one fucks with what's mine." He turns to face me.

The darkness from outside surrounds us and the lights from his car illuminate the godlike features of his face. Suddenly I am speechless and can't breathe.

I picture him leaning over and grabbing my face with his large hands. Pulling me towards him with aggression and sticking his tongue into my mouth. I would moan and tell him how I would be a good girl from now on and no more knife fights in the house.

He clears his throat, pulling me out of my fantasy and reminding me that I need to give him directions, so I put the address to Nick's house. It's close to mine. I would die of embarrassment if he saw where I actually live. As soon as I hit enter, the map appears on the dash.

I sit back and pray that this car drives as fast as it looks so I can end this nightmare of a day. I hope Lincoln doesn't try to make any moves on me because I am not sure I can contain myself. Hopefully, he will keep his beautiful hands to himself.

This girl is fucking with my head. Goddamn, is she a fucking goddess with her face still splattered with that fuckface's blood. She has no idea, and I sure as fuck ain't going to tell her to clean it up.

And my dick fucking concurs.

All he is thinking about is how soon we can work our magic on this one and get her to fuck us with blood all over her fuck able body. Ok, maybe not tonight because she is not like the rest of my fucks, and I want to be able to put even more blood on her body at some point. Not hers, of course...the blood of my enemies.

My kitten is a firecracker when pushed to her limit but a doe-eyed innocent beauty when submissive. Soon after we merged onto the highway, she let her hair down. Something about needing to put it back up since it was all over the place. Didn't bother me. I liked her all fucked up and dirty.

But when those long blonde strands came crashing down along her shoulders, I wanted to slam my black McLaren 720S off to the side of the road so that I could grab ahold and pull them by the handful from her delicate scalp. She would moan and ask me to stop or just take it like my good girl. I am leaning more towards the latter in this case.

Just thinking about the whimpers she would make and the tears that would flow from her beautiful green eyes makes my dick strain painfully in my jeans.

Fuck...

I move in my seat as I shift gears for some relief. The smell of vanilla hits my nose, and it must be coming from her hair. I see that the drive is only 10 more minutes till we approach her house. I need to find out what I can from her while I have her still in my possession.

I told Derek to put Tyler on our tail. I wanted him to see what he could get from peering outside her residence. I knew she didn't go to our college in town or my high school because I would have seen her before tonight.

I need to find her weaknesses, only then can I figure out how to get her willing. If that doesn't work, then I will just take it. But at least I can try to gain her affection first; I am not that much of an asshole. I do enjoy a good challenge from time to time.

"So, do you want to tell me what Fuck Face did back there?" I pause and then look to find her glaring back at me. "What?" I shrug. "I can't ask what he did, but you can come and drop drama on my front door?" I smirk at her, trying to let her feel at ease with my banter.

"I would rather not talk about it if that is ok with you," she says softly and turns to look out her window.

"Ok..." I decide on a different approach. "What about where you go to school?"

After a few moments pass, she sighs, "I go to Riverdale High."

Ah, she goes to public school and the worst part of town, no less. That would make some sense, given her aggressive behavior. I knew of some kids that went there, and most would end up in the hospital. That school had the lowest test scores and highest dropout rates nearby.

"When do you graduate then?" She waits for two beats before answering.

"It's my last year," she says while staring out her window. "I hope that I can get out a little earlier with the way some of my grades are, but not sure. I think I still need to meet with some of my teachers and work on some extracurricular shit as well. I don't know, honestly," she pauses and eyes me suspiciously, "Is this really what you want to talk about?"

Fuck no, this is not what I want to talk about. I would much rather listen to the cute little noises she makes as I finger fuck her until she cums so hard she forgets her own name.

"I just want to learn more about you, is all. I assume you know who I am since you busted into my house this evening, and

I am just trying to have a conversation. I am intrigued by you and just want to know more."

"Intrigued?" She lifts her eyebrow at me.

"Yes. Very intrigued," I smirk.

The ding of the GPS alerts us that we have arrived.

Right away, I know this is not her house. This two-story respectable-looking home is not where my kitten lives. No, my little firecracker doesn't come from the suburbs. My girl is a fighter.

I pull to the curb and put the gear shift in park. Allie tries to figure out how to open the door. It's adorable watching her get so flustered. "Here, let me." I lean over over, push the button that opens the Butterfly wing, and and get another look at her face up close.

Fuck.

I see some blood drops have dripped down on her neck, and I want to lick her clean. I want to push my fingers knuckle deep into her tight, warm walls and feel her nails break the skin on my back.

Allie looks from my eyes to my lips and back again. I start to lean in further for a kiss, and she rushes out of the car before I can.

Goddamn it.

Just like that, she is heading towards the front of the house. I don't wait for her to enter, and I don't run after her little cute ass. I know I need to gain her trust some more, and I won't push it tonight.

My dick had other plans, of course, and curses me the whole fucking ride back home. I call Tyler to ask him if my hunch was right. Sure enough, Tyler confirmed what I suspected.

Once I left her sight, she took off across the road and through the forest to the neighboring trailer park. Tyler followed her until she entered a rundown trailer on the far end of the park.

'Vicarious' by Tool is playing through the sound system when I see a call coming in from Derek.

"Yo man...what do you want me to do with this girl down here? She keeps saying you told her to wait, but dude, we really want to play some fucking pool."

Oh yeah, I had forgotten about her. I tell him to get rid of her. I am not interested in anyone other than Allie. The devil sent me a gift tonight, and I intend on enjoying it fully.

I grabbed my book bag off the crumby brown stained carpet and stormed out the door. I only have the clothes on my back to wear today. My denim jacket is three years old, and you can see my black bra through my white shirt. But that's all I got, so it will have to do.

Mom didn't come home last night, again, but I couldn't worry about where she was at the moment. Probably sleeping off her hangover at some dude's house she stayed with.

Whatever, I am over her bullshit anyways. I can't change her, and I never could.

Once my dad left us 5 years ago, it's just been her going from one crazy asshole to the next. And yes, most of them have tried to make passes at me, and yes, some of them have succeeded.

I didn't want to do the things they tried on me, but I had no choice. I was 13 when my father left me and my alcoholic mother alone for the rest of the world to take advantage of. The selfish bastard knew the world sucked because he was part of it as well.

My first sexual experience happened when I was 14 when my mother's new boyfriend, Carl, wanted to 'help me' get into my bathing suit for the family picnic. I knew it wasn't right, but he had been grooming me for a full year. So I let him...and then I let him push me down to my knees and give me a good solid lesson on sucking cock.

It was disgusting, violent, and messy, but my pussy loved every fucking minute of it. I don't know why....maybe because I was getting attention from a male figure for the first time in a long time. Maybe I felt like I just wanted to make him happy. Maybe I was a fucking young, naive girl who just got taken advantage of. Either way, it is what happened.

Soon after that, Carl would creep into my bed at night and want me to masturbate in front of him. He said he wanted me to orgasm, and if I tried to fake it, he would know. If I were caught faking it, he would brutalize my mother. At the time, I loved my mother and felt sorry for her, so I tried my hardest to get off. The nights I didn't cum fast enough for him, he would rub my small tits and twist my nipples painfully. He would spit in my face and call me a whore until I came hard. I was ashamed, so I finally got the nerve to tell my mother.

I told my mom after Carl took my virginity at 16. She told me that it was my fault. I had talked too sweetly to him and always wanted his attention. That evening, Carl proceeded to fuck my ass for the first time; he didn't prep me or go easy. Soon after, he got in trouble with some gamblers and left. We never heard from him again, and I hope he is buried somewhere in the desert.

"Hey Allie Cat!" I hear Nick yell from across the street. Nick Peterson lives on the other side of the park, hidden behind the massive set of forests in my backyard.

I didn't want Lincoln to see where I really lived. He was used to girls who smelled of Chanel #5 and wore thousand-dollar flip flops or some shit. Not girls like me from the trash and dirt.

"Hey Nick…how things been?" I yell back as I make my way up to his house. Getting a ride from his street is much easier than trying to get one out of the park. But today, I was just walking the rest of the way to work.

The bookstore was the only one in town for miles and was family-owned. Mrs. Jackson had basically given it to me to manage while she stayed home. Approaching 90 years old, she didn't have the energy to get out much, but she knew I enjoyed running things for her. It's a great experience, and I could possibly use it on my college applications.

Nick falls in step next to me as I throw my hair up into a high ponytail. I hope he doesn't bring up his hoodie that I had to destroy so he didn't get in trouble for assaulting Brett by accident. Brett…that asshole better be hurting today, and I hope his entire football career is over. What he did to Stephanie was unforgivable.

Nick grabs my shoulder, stopping me from entering traffic right before a car flies by, almost killing me.

"Whoa, Allie…watch where you're going, sweetie." I feel my heartbeat go back to normal and give him a faint smile.

"Sorry, just lost in my thoughts."

Nick is nice enough with hazel brown eyes and blonde hair. He is cute but not my type. We all know my type, and he is tall, dark, devilishly handsome, and trouble, trouble, trouble.

Fuck. Ever since Lincoln dropped me off last night, I have not stopped thinking about him. When he leaned in to open my door, I felt like he might kiss me, and I wanted him to. But then I quickly thought, what could he possibly want from a girl like me except to fuck me and leave me for dead? I'm sure I am not his type. And most importantly, I am sure he has his pick of the litter when it comes to willing girls.

"Hey, are you listening to me?" Nick's voice interrupts me again. I stop in front of the bookstore. Oh shit, what was the last thing he said to me?

"Sorry, Nick, I have just a lot on my mind." I slide the key into the hole and cross the threshold. I notice the time and realize I have 5 minutes to get the store opened. I know that it's not like a line has formed outside or anything, but I still like to be prompt.

Nick follows me inside, right on my heels. "Lost in your thoughts and a lot on your mind, huh?" he says with a hint of bite in his tone.

With any other person, I would tell them to wait outside, but I have known Nick ever since my dad left, so he's always been a big brother of sorts to me. I lock the door back behind me and go straight to the office in the back room. I go to the safe and put in the combination. Mrs. Jackson is so sentimental. The code is her wedding anniversary. Her husband died two years ago.

I grab the till and start to count the money. Even though I closed last night, I still like to stick to my habits. I guess Nick has something really important to talk to me about since he continues hovering over me across from the small desk. I grab what I need and head out towards the front of the store.

After getting all situated with the cash register, I look over to find Nick still loitering. He stands on the other side of the counter and patiently waits for me to notice him.

"Ok, ok..sorry, you have my full attention now," I smile.

"Ok..so here is the thin-"

"OH shit! Let me go unlock the door first!" I shout and run around the counter heading towards the front. I hear his laughter behind me as I flip the store's sign to read 'Open'. I pocket the store's keys.

"Yeah, wouldn't want to keep any of those crazy readers begging for more books." I roll my eyes and turn back towards him.

"Yeah yeah, real funny, smart ass. Ok, so what is it that you wanted to talk to me about?" I cross my arms, waiting for whatever is on his mind.

Nick walks to me until he is standing toe to toe. I get a wheezy feeling in my stomach. He wears too much cologne. I don't know why I didn't smell it before but it invades my nostrils now. I feel a cough crawling up my throat but hold it in.

"I just wanted to tell you that I think we should stop pussyfooting around this thing that has been going on with us forever and give it a shot," he says confidently and runs his hands down my arms. I feel nauseous and back myself up abruptly.

I see in his eyes the disappointment. This is not the reaction he had hoped for, and nervously, runs his hands through his hair. His long-sleeved shirt rises up, showcasing his taught muscles above his jeans.

He is a sweetheart. He is attractive, yet he does nothing for me physically. Sure, I could go out with him and pretend to be enjoying myself, but I would always feel like lying to him and myself. He is just too nice of a person to do that to, and I know he will find the right girl…it just isn't me.

I am ruined. I am not meant for him.

"I am real sorry, Nick. I just don't see you in that way…you have always been there for me, and I love you like a broth-"

He cuts me off this time. "Like a brother," he says with defeat. "Yeah, I know." He pushes his hands deep in his pockets. "I get it. I can be patient until you realize the truth about us. This could be a good thing, Allie. Just please think about it?" He brushes past me, heading towards the door.

He doesn't get it, but I don't have the energy to do this right now. I have too many things to worry about, and I can't be distracted. He should know this about me, but he doesn't because he has a misconception of me. He only sees what he wants to see. And what he sees is a pitiful little girl with daddy issues.

The Saturday had been slow, but as I start to clean up the books that were out of place, I hear the chime above the door. I look at my watch and notice it's 5 past the hour. I guess I forgot to lock the door when I headed back to the Romance section. We had gotten a small shipment, and I picked up one that looked interesting. I got lost in reading and forgot to check the time.

"Sorry, we are closed, but you can come back Monday when we open again," I yell over my shoulder as I push in the remaining book I held in my arms. Perfect fit. I love it when things just work out.

When I turn around, I slam right into a hard chest. Then I smell him as it engulfs my nostrils. Floral.

"Fuck!" I gasp out loud as I hold my chest.

Lincoln stands in front of me, staring down into my eyes. I lose my thoughts, I lose my breath, I lose my stomach, and I can't stop staring.

"What if I don't want to come back on Monday?" He teases and places a smirk on the side of his face. My panties get wet, and I try to back up but just end up running into the shelf.

"Owe!" I massage my funny bone and attempt to calm down. "What are you doing here?" I ask harsher than I meant to.

He pushes his hands into his front pockets like Nick did, but Lincoln's movements look intended and not out of nervousness. His jeans dip once his hands are firmly in his pockets, revealing the top part of his boxer briefs. I caught the white briefs with Burberry stretched across in black letters. They probably cost more than my monthly gas bill.

I catch an outline of a black tattoo that looks like it goes up his torso, but I only get a glimpse.

"Now, is that how you greet all of your customers, Miss Parker?" His smooth voice sends shivers down to my toes. I swallow down what I can in my mouth and try to put on a strong front. I drop my hands to my sides and straighten my back.

"Well, truth be told, you are coming in after closing, so I technically have the right to throw you out," I say with some force I conjured up from somewhere and cross my arms.

A deep chuckle rises from his chest as he throws his head back, extremely amused.

"I would fucking love you see you try, baby."

And then I feel the gush of arousal in my panties, again.

I don't have time for a rebuttal because he slaps his hands together and ushers me towards the front. "Come on...I am taking you out." He strolls past me like he owns the fucking place.

"Wait, what?" I try to keep up with him, but his long strides are nothing compared to my petite legs. He flies through the aisles as if he memorized all the exits to this place. He grabs the store keys lying on the front counter. He reaches the door, flips the sign back over to 'Closed' and firmly locks it.

Lincoln turns to me and leans back slowly till his back hits the door with a light thud. He crosses his arms and ankles while staring at me. For the first time, I now notice his big forearms and biceps. Shit...he is much more muscular than I thought.

"Don't want to get any more unwanted customers to stalk in now, would we?" A mischievous grin rises on his face, and my insides drop for the second time in 5 seconds. He stands guard, waiting for my response.

"Ok...let me just finish closing up, ok?" Why I ask for his acceptance, I have no idea. It's as if he rips my obedience from me without permission. He looks at me, and I want to please him. I want to get down on my filthy knees and pray to him. I want to worship at his pristine feet and greedily take anything he allows me to have.

God fucking help me. What did I just say to myself?

Lincoln

Fucking adorable.

This is what I think of Allie Parker.

And now I am pretty sure I have never used that word to describe anything other than her...ever. I have never cared if something was adorable before her. I only cared if it was useful to me or not. Allie is possibly the most useful thing I have ever wanted.

She is afraid but also intrigued by my little unexpected visit. I watch her walk around the store finishing up her closing duties like the good girl that she is, and my dick twitches in my pants. My mind, nor my dick, have stopped thinking about her since we dropped her off last night.

I hear the switches clicking in the back and see each row of lights flicker off. She walks towards me wearing short blue jean shorts, black boots, a white t-shirt, and a jean jacket. The jacket definitely looks too small, but she doesn't seem to care.

What I fucking love the most is that she wears a basic black bra that you can see right through the thin fabric of her t-shirt.

God. Damn.

I can't wait till those tits are in my fucking hands. I would squeeze and twist her nipples so hard that her cries would be a sweet mixture of pain and pleasure. I'll finger fuck her till she is coming all over my hand. Then, I will make her suck my fingers, tasting her cum, licking them like a fucking junkie, and telling me repeatedly how she wants to please me and only me — how she will be my good girl but only for me.

As she strolls closer, I see her beautiful features even more. The lights from across the street have turned on. The soft glow shows off her blonde highlights, but what I want to see is the darkness below it. I want her dark depravity.

She stops in front of me, waiting for me to move aside. She doesn't say it, though; she just waits for me to move first.

Good girl.

Once I step aside, she rushes to the door. I smell her sweet vanilla hair, and I'm tempted to pull on her ponytail just a bit. Just a tease. But I don't...soon, soon enough, she will know who she belongs to.

The wind picks up as we step outside. I walk around to the passenger side and open it up for her. She strides right up to it like the fucking goddess that she is and smiles.

"Don't lock your car either, hmm? So badass don't need to do that?" She teases.

This fucking girl. She has no idea the effect she has on me.

I motion for her to slide inside and walk around back to come around. I step in and drop the doors. I turned over the powerful engine and looked over at her. I get lost in her green eyes for two beats.

As I slowly draw up my hand, I see her pulse quicken. I cup her cheek in my large palm. I feel her slightly leaning into me. Then, I whisper against her mouth, "I told you, Babygirl, no one fucks with what's mine." I release my hold on her and lean back in my seat. I tap her nose with my finger and shift the car into first gear.

What the fuck have I gotten myself into.

Goddamn!

I sure as hell was not expecting Lincoln to pick me up from work, and I sure as fuck wasn't expecting him to take me out to a fancy dinner. The looks I am getting in this place would make the Queen of England feel intimidated. I instantly feel like I don't belong here. The judgment is obvious on all faces I see, even the ones who work here. I am so out of my element. The menu is in French, for fuck's sake. But I guess it doesn't matter because Lincoln went ahead and ordered for us, fluently in French, might I add.

And now my panties are fucking soaked.

Again.

Yes, you read that correctly…it's as if a dam broke loose, and now the floodgates have opened.

Welcome to the party, my friends. My pussy is weeping for your enjoyment.

It started when he surrounded me in the bookstore, and then he had to put his hands on me in the car. I don't feel safe with him because he makes me lose all my defenses against manipulative men like himself.

I knew it as soon as we walked into this fancy ass restaurant. The way he acted towards these rich assholes was not the version of him that I got back in the bookstore.

This Lincoln is a polite, sweet talker, friendly, hand-shaking good o'boy. The Lincoln I know is a dark, mysterious, and dangerous man . I wonder what lies inside of his dark soul.

I get bold sitting so close to him and ask, "So, is it difficult being a Reynolds?" I say with a little bit of sass. He lazily looks over and runs his eyes up and down my face for the 100th time.

"Maybe you'll find out someday."

The seriousness in his tone has me spitting and choking on my ice water. He pats me harshly on the back as I cough and try to get back some of the composure I just lost.

I clear my throat and take another sip, but it doesn't seem to help because all I can feel is Lincoln's hand slowly starting to run up and down my back. I feel his touch through my thin shirt and jacket.

I am suddenly hot again, as when we pulled up to this extravagant restaurant. The valet was there to get me out of Lincoln's confusing car, but it was Lincoln who held out his hand to me. Once it was in mine, I felt the heat run through my body like an electric current. He smiled and pulled me alongside him like we were a happy couple.

The hostess greeted him with seductive eyes, and her face instantly lit up at the sight of him. She wore a tight black dress and her hair was done up in an even tighter blonde bun.

"Mr. Reynolds. It is so nice to see you again."

She dropped her gaze to eye me from head to toe. She looked like she was two seconds from asking me if I needed her to call the local church to see if they had a bed for me tonight.

Lincoln let her know it would be just us for dinner. His hand landed on my hip, and I felt his fingers dig into my side. The hostess pursed her lips together and then smiled, leading us away. I gulped what little saliva I had, and Lincoln ushered me to follow her.

She led us to a table in the center of the room where everyone had a front-seat ticket to see me in all my humiliated glory. When the hostess began to spout out the specials, Lincoln interrupted her. He pointed at a far, dark, half-circled booth in the corner and stated he wanted that one instead. Lincoln didn't wait for her response as he sauntered over towards our table, expecting people to follow. And, of course, we did.

However, as soon as his words came out implying that he would marry me one day, I just lost my shit. I was now trying to recover from a different type of humiliation.

I laughed, once I could swallow without my throat feeling like the Sahara Desert and looked him in the eyes.

"Right. Ha. That is funny, Lincoln. I didn't know you were such a comedian too, ya know."

"Link."

"Huh?" I cleared my throat again.

"You can call me Link. Everyone else does." He shrugs and takes a sip of his drink.

"Not everyone. I seem to remember a certain hostess that preferred to call you..oh what was it...oh yeah...Mr. Reynolds." I giggle but then see the tension in his prominent jaw.

"Yeah well...I don't care for that one much either." He slams his drink on the counter with a heavy thud. Dismissing my blatant jealousy.

"So, how do you like college?" I decided to change gears and go towards a safer route.

He eyes me considerably before speaking. He waits, and I feel my body heat rising. Being back in the corner, I do feel like I could comfortably take off my jacket, but I'm not sure I really want to. And again, I didn't think I would be feeling so naked just by the way he looked at me.

"You really want to know, or do you want to know what I tell everyone who asks me?" Lincoln turns his body more towards me as he leans in closer to my face.

"I want you to always tell me the truth," I say softly, searching his blue eyes in the hope he can sense my sincerity.

His hand comes up to lightly grab a strand of my hair and tuck it behind my ear. He leans further in, dropping his gaze to my lips and whispers. "It's a fucking joke, is what it is. I'm enrolled in college, yes, and I go enough for the faculty not to raise hell." He starts to run his long fingers up my inner thigh, and I feel his hot breath on my face.

"The ones who care, I mean, and can't be bought with my father's money," he huffs. "The others, though, don't give a fuck, so I just attend a couple of courses. It's all fixed…I just get the flimsy paper so I can say I did it, but that's not the end game for me."

Slowly, he draws his hand further up to the edge of my shorts. I grab his wrist just as he is about to push up further, "Don't," I say with a forceful voice I didn't know I had in me. It was on instinct to stop him. Another who will just take advantage of me and my fucked-up situation.

He stops his ascent to my center. I look up into his hooded eyes. His hair is falling forward, and it looks so soft, but I can't do this. I am not this girl…I do not fuck someone in front of a room full of assholes eating entrees that cost more than my bills for a full month.

"Excuse me." I go to stand and grab my bag feeling the need to get the fuck out of this situation and fast.

I feel his hand on my wrist and a slight twist. I wince from the pain, and he pulls me down forcefully.

Lincoln pulls my back against his chest. I feel his breath on the back of my neck. I don't look at him. My heart rate is pounding, and my breathing is erratic. I can feel my heartbeat in my ears. I can't stop the pooling in my panties, and I can't stop this train from crashing into a huge fucking landmine.

Lincoln

Fuck, she has got some goddamn nerve trying to get away from me. Sure, I may have pushed it a little with trying to get a feel but come the fuck on...I have been a patient fucking man sitting over here starving, metaphorically and physically.

I wanted to bring her to dinner because that is what nice guys do...right? They take their girl out to dinner, and then they get to fuck her brains out all night long while listening to her cry their name out repeatedly.

That is why I tried to get a fucking feel because I am not used to waiting, and I am damn sure not used to being told no. So, when her little ass tries to stand up from this table, I draw the fucking line in the sand. She needs to learn sooner rather than later. But I can't because I must play this one right for fucks sake. She will fight...she will run. Or try to run.

"Listen, Allie...I am sorry, ok?" I try to put on my most genuine, caring voice I can. I moved away from her to allow her some space. I fucking hate it, but I allow it because she was a good girl and sat down when I made her.

She watches me. Skeptical of my motives, as she should be.

50/50 chance at this point she believes my bullshit or doesn't. To sweeten the deal, I give her my panty-dropping smile, asking again for her forgiveness.

This is the face I give to all of my father's little stuck-up bitches he brings around. All of his charity events and political galas that he forces my attendance to always bring out the cougars, and they love nothing more than a spoiled little rich boy to rock their night. And I happily did that up till Allie Parker came slamming into my life.

Fuck…now I gotta try to be that sweet talker all over again. For now, anyways…

"Look, it's just difficult for me being with you and not being able to put my hands on you, ok?" I shrug in defeat. She appears to still not trust me, so I proceed. "What I mean to say is that I really like you. I don't like many people, but I like you. It's true that no one really knows the real me, but I would like you to get to know me better. And in essence, I get to know you better," I plead.

I never fucking plead.

I look at her face trying to gauge if I need to move forward with more bullshit or if it's enough for now. I mean, it's not entirely bullshit; it's just not my primary motive.

"Ok, but that was a warning," she seethes.

Fucking adorable.

"Don't put your hands on me, Link, or I will leave." I love her little defiant speech. Oh, baby, you will learn who is in charge and who has always been in charge since we met.

"You got it. Hands to myself." I wink, and she rolls her eyes.

And just like that, we're back in fucking business.

Fuck was it only last night she came into my life? Damn, the day got away from me...probably because I had Tyler give me a full rundown earlier when he got back from tailing her. I couldn't keep my thoughts away from her.

When Tyler stepped foot into my father's office, I couldn't wait to hear all the details about my little kitten. I hoped she would go home, look at herself in the mirror, and instantly rub one out just by looking at her beautiful, savage face. Her plumb cherry lips and her soft fucking breasts...I mean, I haven't seen them or felt them, but I know those are fucking perfect for me. Tyler came to report to me as soon as she was safe and sound at her little bookstore.

"Well, she lives in a doublewide with her mom and her dad left when she was 13." Tyler stands across from me now. "And from what the neighbors say, her mom isn't there a whole lot. Also sounds like when she is home, there is a lot of yelling. She seems to be an alcoholic and likes to bring random guys over." What the fuck?

I need names, and if any of those motherfuckers touched what belongs to me, they are dead. I don't care if she wasn't mine before last night...she's mine now, and that fucking counts.

"Anything else?" I sigh, leaning back on the high back chair and placing my dirty boots on my father's rare mahogany desk.

"Yeah...there is a boyfriend." I stop flicking my zippo and shove it into my front pocket.

I look back over to Tyler and slowly stand up. "What you mean a fucking boyfriend?"

He shifts from one foot to the next. "I don't know, Link. Some dude walked with her to the bookstore and went inside." He shoves his hands into his jacket.

"Did he touch her?" I take a deep breath, reminding myself that Tyler's orders were to watch and not engage. But fuck he could have fucking given me a call.

"I couldn't tell. It was hard to see inside the shop from my vantage point, and I couldn't see shit when they went in the back room..." I grab the closest thing I can find on my father's desk and throw it against the wall. It's the Tiffany Co. picture frame of my dad hugging his third wife while skiing in Aspen. It shatters into a million pieces on the hardwood floors.

I inhale and exhale. Get it the fuck together, Link. "What did you see?" I ask calmly. I am half the size of Tyler, but he knows better than to try fuck with me when I am in this mood.

He shifts uncomfortably. "Well, I saw he met up with her in front of that house you dropped her off at. I guess he lives there or some shit."

I walk around to lean against the front of the desk, now motioning for Tyler to sit so that I can look down at him. He drops down into the leather chair and rests his ankle on the opposite knee. "Then he walked next to her, talking while she seemed to be uninterested. I mean, she almost got hit by a car even." my jaw tightens. "Then he followed her into the store. About 10 minutes later, he walked out, and that was it."

"That was it?" I question to see if he is leaving anything out. My feelings, with regards to trust, are non-existent.

My father taught me that valuable lesson at my 10th birthday party. He told me to invite all my friends and their families over to our house for my big celebration. If it had been up to me, I would have just had Derek and Tyler over to play basketball, but my father had other intentions.

The party was what you would expect from a disturbingly rich kid. Our backyard had been turned into a literal zoo with all sorts of animals. There were monkeys, giraffes, and elephants, and we even had a lion and tiger. The zookeepers allowed kids to come up and touch or feed some of the animals. I didn't care much for any of it till the lions and tigers got to be fed. That shit was a fucking rush to see. All the blood and carnage got my prepubescent dick hard.

As soon as they were about to throw some meat to the tiger, I was tapped on the shoulder by Kevin Stanson, my father's righthand man at the time. "Your father wants to see you in his office. Alone."

"But the fireworks are starting soon." I didn't give a fuck about the fireworks. I just wanted to stay with the big cats.

"Now, young Lincoln. He won't wait long." He put his heavy hand on my shoulder and squeezed to emphasize the meaning.

I was fuming by the time I got to my father's office door, so much so that I didn't even bother to knock. I stormed in, determined to yell at my father for summoning me, but the wind was knocked out of me when I saw what was before me.

A middle-aged man was tied to a chair in the middle of my father's office. His body was hunched over, spit mixed with blood was drooling out of his mouth. His face was bruised and swollen. I looked over to see my father standing before this man, holding a lead pipe.

"Lincoln, my boy, this is your birthday present." My father's words released me from my trance. He patted me on the back, and I glanced at his sadistic smile spreading on his face. "Your first kill."

Pulling myself out of the memory, I ask Tyler. "How did he look when he left versus how he went in?"

"To be honest, man…he looked sad. Like his fucking puppy just died." He laughs to break the tension stewing in the air.

Shit ain't funny.

"Find out everything you can on him," I tell Tyler to dismiss him from my sight.

Soon after that, I decided I needed to see her. I needed to stake a claim fast before any other fuck faces tried to move in on her.

"Would you like some dessert?" The waitress asks me in French. It's not lost on me that Allie pushes her thighs together when I respond back to her in French.

Now that I have her back in my good graces, I can maybe try to find out about this "boyfriend." As soon as the dessert hit the table, I dropped my black card. It was time to get the fuck out of here. I had plans with my little deviant, and I wanted to start playing, but first, I needed to know about this fucker.

I waited till we got back to my house before I asked the question I had been dying to ask her since I got her little ass in my hands. I turn off the engine, lift the doors, and look over at her.

"Who is Nick?"

Instantly, her cheeks flush, and her eyebrows frown. I don't like it.

Not one fucking bit.

"Um, how do you know about Nick?"

"I have my ways," I shrug.

She seems curious about me, and I can see the wheels turning in her beautiful head. Before she jumps off towards the deepest part of the ocean, I try to save myself. "I meant I was worried about you last night, thinking that Brett may want revenge for the brutal savagery you inflicted upon him." My dick twitches.

"So, you followed me?" She sighs and draws her eyebrows further in.

"No."

Technically, I was not the one to follow her.

"Mhmm" is all she gives me. I can tell she is getting angrier by the second.

"Ok...ok...yes, I had you followed, but honestly, it was for your own good. Brett is a pussy, but he could still do some dumb shit like go after you thinking his rich daddy will bail him out."

"Oh god," she suddenly dumps her head in her hands. "Fuck! I forgot all about who his daddy even is!!"

She exits the car quickly and starts flinging her hands in the air up and down like a new bird trying to learn to fly. "That's it...I am done for. He will want to press charges, and then I am never getting out of this fucking shit hole. God! Fuck! I am going to end up like my mother, and that's that... it's over for me." She is pacing back and forth now. "Goodbye college. Goodbye, white picket fences and dogs and soccer practices and birthday parties…or whatever the American dream is because I sure as hell am never going to see it!"

Done with this bullshit, I come around my car and grab both cheeks in my hands. I turn her face to stare into my eyes. God, she is the most beautiful creature I have ever seen.

I search her green eyes and tell her with certainty, "It's going to be alright. I will take care of it for you."

And I will.

I already have the motions in play. She just doesn't need to know about it yet. Allie takes a deep breath in and lets it out her cute button nose.

"How are you going to do that, huh?"

I still don't know what fuck face did, but truth be told, I don't give one flying fuck. He pissed off my girl, and that is enough for me.

"You let me worry about that." I lean down to brush my lips over hers but stop and hold. It isn't until I feel her fall forward into me the slightest bit that I pull back. I smile and interlace her fingers with mine. I led her towards the front door. Now, she is home. Now, she is with me. Now, we are alone. And now, my toy and I can finally play.

I walk into the massive house again and notice how very different the place appears versus how it was last night. The house isn't lit up as much as it was last night, and it's very quiet as we walk into the kitchen. No blaring music, no drunk frat boys, no judgy girls eyeing me, just Lincoln and I in this big ol'house.

"You can leave your stuff over there." He motions over to the couch that sits off the kitchen area. "No one is home, so we have the whole place to ourselves." He grins and holds out both arms. It's then that I see just how big he truly is.

I can't catch my breath and ask to see the bathroom fast enough. Lincoln points his arm to the left and turns toward the fridge. He starts to rummage through, looking for things as I head down the hall.

I have never been in a house this size before this weekend, but I love the smell. I see fresh flowers all over, so I assume that must be where the overpowering scent that Lincoln harbors comes from.

Getting involved with Lincoln Reynolds is not going to happen, and it should not happen because he is fucking crazy. I know what I have gotten myself into, and it's not good, but when he said he could help me with this Brett issue, then maybe I could use a friend like him. I mean, come on; other people use their friends to get shit done. It's called networking...yeah, I looked it up even. Read a whole book on it, too, that we got in a shipment at the store once.

Exasperated, I opened up my purse and pulled out my baggie of Xanax. I am down to my last two. I will need to see if I can get some from somewhere since I stole these from my mother's stash.

I take one while grabbing a handful of water from the faucet. I throw my head back to wash it down and feel wetness on my shirt. Great, Allie...I guess you thought you were entering a wet t-shirt contest today, too.

Perfect.

I grab a towel from the ones that are stacked like a pyramid on the counter. I attempt to dry my shirt, but there is no point. I try to pull my denim jacket closed to cover up, but it's useless. The damn thing needs to be thrown out, but I am low on clothing.

I finish my business and wash my hands. I dry them off with the hand towel, attempt to roll it back up, and place it promptly on the stack. It doesn't look as perfect as it did before but fuck it.

When I open the door, I am fully prepared to go out to the kitchen and tell Lincoln to take me home. The Xanax should be taking effect any minute, and I feel like I can confront the allure that follows Lincoln Reynolds.

However, I was not prepared to slam into his hard chest for the second time tonight. I look up into his dark eyes. He has that predatory look again that he gives me sometimes.

"Did you miss me, baby?" He drawls out, looking at my chest.

Fuck what his tone and voice does to me. "I, uh, I was just coming to find you."

"Oh yeah," he says as he starts walking towards me, causing me to fall back into the bathroom and the sink. I feel like a meek little mouse caught by the big scary cat.

"Well, you found me," his smooth voice states. His eyes glance down at my mouth, and I lick my dry lips.

"Did you get your shirt all wet for me, baby?" He grazes his eyes up and down my perky chest. Then his hand comes up and grabs ahold of my tender throat. His grip is firm and intentional.

I can't speak. He has a hold of my airways. I can't break eye contact with him, either. My pussy drips with anticipation of what his lips and mouth could do. He licks his lips as if he could read my mind and lowers his head to reach my ear. He nips my earlobe in his mouth and whispers, "Mine." I moan in response and realize I am fucked.

My eyes close instinctually, and Lincoln's other hand comes up to grab my hair, pulling until I wince from the pain. I let out a whimper as he kisses my neck. He slowly trails his tongue up the side of my neck and stops below my ear. "You are so fucking perfect, Allie."

I can barely hold myself up, but when he says that. I grab ahold of his black, loose-fitting t-shirt to keep me grounded.

"Please."

For fuck's sake, Allie, begging already, are we?

Lincoln chuckles into my ear confirming that he knows exactly what I was thinking. He lets go of my throat to grab onto my ass, palming it so hard I feel a bruise will show tomorrow, and I can't fucking wait to see it.

"Like I said, fucking perfect." He whispers across my mouth.

I push my hips into his hard cock as I whimper again against his chest, desperately trying to get some friction. I just need a touch...a tongue...lips...fucking anything right now on my willing body. He pulls on my hair a bit harder as I rub up against him.

"Fuck," he shoves me up against the wall, picking me up by my thighs. His hardness is lined up perfectly to hit my spot, so I try to shove against him harder.

Fuck, I am like a wild fucking animal; I just need more.

"Allie...I am going to fuck you so hard you won't remember your fucking name let alone some asshole who thinks he can fucking touch you."

What? What the fuck is he talking about right now? How can he be thinking about anything else at this moment?

"What?" I say, breathless and exasperated. I run my fingers through his coffee-colored hair, and it feels exactly how I thought it would feel; precisely like cashmere-covered clouds.

"Lincoln...what the fuck are you talking about?"

It's then that I finally see his eyes again since they have been buried deep within my collarbone. Lincoln stands back, dropping me on my booted feet with a thud. I try to gather myself, but all I can feel is the loss of his warm body up against mine and how much I want it back. My brows frown inward, and I whimper.

Just as I am about to jump back on him, with no shame, he kisses me. He grabs the hair at the nape of my neck, pulling me harshly. This time, I truly cry out in pain, but again, my pussy clenches because she is a fucking crazy bitch.

His tongue enters my mouth, and I open for him with everything I have. His tongue plays with mine expertly back and forth. He starts out passionately, but then it turns into something else completely different. His kiss is hard and possessive, as if he wants to mark me from the inside out.

"You, Allie Parker, are mine. And remember what I said about what's mine?" Just as his words hit me, he slams his mouth into me again.

His tongue is vicious as it enters my mouth, claiming every inch for himself. I moan and continue to grab ahold of him anywhere and everywhere. God, damn, I knew he was all brute strength, but I had no idea his body felt like this. He is a brick wall of flesh and bone. Pushing me to the brink of insanity. My head is fuzzy, and my body is heavy.

I feel lightheaded as my body craves oxygen. I grabbed the back of his neck, pulling him into me even more. At this moment, I feel I would willingly give Lincoln my last breath if he requested it of me.

His palms cup my face, and he pulls me in against him. His hard cock is now resting against my stomach. My hands, having a mind of their own, eagerly go for his belt.

He grabs ahold of my hands and shakes his head. "No, baby. Not here."

He steps back from me but doesn't break the hold on my hands. He pulls me out of the bathroom and leads me upstairs. It seems like it takes an eternity to get where we are going, but I don't mind since I get to admire Lincoln's swagger as he pulls me along to an unknown destination. His heavy feet clunk on the hardwood floors as mine are just trying to keep up with his long strides.

We finally get to a door, and he opens it. I stop at the entrance, looking over the view in front of me.-This must be his bedroom.

The back wall is nothing but windows that overlook a vast forest. As soon as I get carried away with seeing how far back the trees go, I hear a humming sound and see covers coming down from the ceiling, hiding the pleasant view. It startles me for a moment, and I hear a low chuckle behind me.

"You are always surprising me you know that, Lincoln Reynolds?" I say with a smile on my face.

He closes the bedroom door with his foot, never breaking eye contact with me. His gaze reminds me of a tiger hunting their prey in a low bush. He seems calculated as he strolls further into the room. I get distracted by the large, canopy king-sized bed to the right of me.

It sits in the middle of the room on a pedestal, for Christ's sake. It is draped in black curtains and black bed sheets. I see extensive ornate decorations that flourish around the dark wood. There are two nightstands on each side but no lamps, no clocks, nothing to add to any personal tastes or preferences. The only light is coming from the bathroom that sits off to the side. It adds a soft glow flowing into the dark, eerie room. I walk towards it to continue my little tour, but then I feel him behind me.

He grabs ahold of my hips and digs his long fingers into my flesh hard. I fall back into him and rub my ass up against his dick. His head falls to my neck. My clit begs for attention and hopes my mind won't fuck it up for her. He slowly drags his hands up under my shirt and squeezes my tits hard. I let out a groan and push back into him harder.

His left hand comes out and grabs a fistful of my hair. He pulls it on so hard that I cry out his name and gush at the same time. I don't know if he can smell the evidence of my arousal from here, but I sure as hell can.

He drags his right hand up further, bringing my shirt up higher until he can grab onto my throat. He squeezes my airway enough for me to have to hold my breath. My head is spinning, and the only thing I can think of is what his hands would feel like rubbing on my clit and fingering my wet insides.

"Please. Please touch me." I say breathlessly.

Lincoln grabs my chin and pulls me back so my eyes meet his. I can barely keep them open with the intense feelings I have running through my body.

"Is that what my baby wants? Do you want to show me how much you belong to me?" And with that he takes his left hand that was holding my hair and pushes past my waistband. He dives behind my panties and shoves two fingers into me without remorse.

His fingers slide in with no protest as I clench around his knuckles. I groan and push my ass back.

"Ah, there she is," he whispers into my ear. "So, fucking wet and already so close, are we, baby?" He chuckles against my neck, and I fucking lose it. I am on the precipice of letting go, but then he retreats his hands completely.

"What the fuck!" I huff out loud. Lincoln steps in front of me and grabs ahold of my chin.

"Don't worry, baby. I am going to make you come harder than you ever have before. But right now…I need you to strip." And with that he slowly starts to step back towards the chair in the corner. I never even knew that it was there.

Lincoln grabs the back of his shirt and rips it off his head, throwing it to the side. Fuck me. I am now seeing what lies underneath. He is a god. A beautiful, dangerous, dark god.

He widens his legs as he sits and grabs a cigarette from his front pocket. He lights it with his black zippo and waits for me to strip. I take off my jacket and drop it behind me. I toed off my boots along with my mismatched socks. I feel the softness of his fuzzy white carpeting between my toes. I had no idea carpets could ever feel like this.

I grab the hem of my wet shirt and pull it off, making sure I tilt my head slightly so my hair falls, cascading over my shoulder. I start to unbutton my jean shorts and wiggle out of them. I stand there in my black bra and black thong. I watch Lincoln's face as he takes me in from my head all the way down to my toes.

"The rest of it." His tone is demanding, but I detect a slight raspiness, too. He takes another drag of smoke and lets it out slowly. Lincoln either commanded the smoke to settle around him or it, just like me, merely wishes to be in his orbit.

I unclasp my bra and drop it in front of me. I drag my fingers down my sides and push the bottoms down. I stand completely naked in front of him, never breaking eye contact.

I wait.

I wait for his instructions.

I wait for his command.

I wait because I am a good girl.

He lays his burning cigarette on the ashtray that sits on top of the adjacent table. He leaves it there to burn as he slowly rises from his throne. Lincoln takes two steps to be in front of me and then cradles my face with his large hands. He slowly starts to drag his right hand down my throat. I watch as his eyes follow his fingers descending my body. He slides them past my collarbone and between my naked breasts. My chest is heaving, up and down, as I try to stand still for him. I can't stop my thighs from rubbing together when his hand finally flattens out at my stomach. He pauses and then snaps his eyes back to my eager ones.

His hand abruptly cups my pussy, and I feel his fingers at my sopping opening. His lips brush mine. I lost all my patience. I dive my tongue into his mouth and let him roll it with his. His moves are methodical. He drives me to the edge and then teases me with anticipation of euphoria. I want him. God, I want him so bad.

"Please, Lincoln. Please. I need it so bad." I beg without shame. He continues to penetrate me with his skillful fingers.

"Awe, baby. You must earn that. Are you ready to earn it?" I look up at him in those deep blue eyes. I am gladly drowning in them.

"Yes," I say, ready to do whatever he wants.

She is better than I could ever fucking imagine. I feel her wetness soaking my hand as I cup her. My pussy. My fucking hole.

"Get on your knees," she does it instantly but then waits for my instructions. We established what a good girl she is, after all.

"Take off my belt." She fumbles with it at first. Her shaky hands give her away. She slides it out slowly until it falls to the floor beside her beautiful, soft body. I nudge my head up to encourage her to keep going. A slight smile forms on her face.

My dick is about to explode as she takes each button of my fly and undoes them slowly, one at a time. She is a fucking tease with her big green eyes looking back up at me. Those plump cherry lips. That fucking mouth is just waiting for my cock. To penetrate. To own. To fucking decimate.

As soon as my dick falls out, I grab the back of her head. She gasps, and my dick twitches.

I leaned down over her. "Stick out your tongue." She does it while maintaining eye contact with me.

My fucking girl.

"Show me who owns you, Allie. Show me that you'll take whatever I give you." I roll my tongue to gather my spit and let it drip from *my* mouth into *hers*.

"Swallow," and she does with a beautiful fucking smile on her face.

"Fuuuck."

Fucking perfect.

She runs her tongue up the length of my cock from root to tip. She drags it up and around till I see precum bubble out.

It's as if the taste of my come rose her from a deep sleep, and she wants to relish in all that is my dick. Deep throating till she is coughing and gagging. I groan and throw my head back.

"Fuuuckkk," I strain out.

I knew she would be it for me. I hold her head down until her eyes water, and those beautiful fucking eyes start to drain tears of pure gold. She never once puts her hands on me in retaliation. I pull back, and she gasps as if she had only moments before passing out from lack of oxygen.

"That's my girl." I stroked her face. "You are so fucking beautiful. Do you know that?"

I pick her up off the floor and throw her on my bed. I pull off my jeans the rest of the way and climb on top.

Enough of that...I need to fuck my pussy and reward her for good behavior. She giggles as I hover over her. God, she has no idea what she has gotten herself into.

I pushed her legs open wider with my knees and settled in. Holding myself up with my forearms, I searched her eyes. "Where did you come from?"

She lifts her head and kisses me lightly on the lips. I was never into kissing before. I mean, what's the fucking point. Maybe if I got off on it, but that never happened.

Mouths are for food and fucking only. That's it.

Now, I can see the appeal. I probably could nut one out just by having her lips on mine and rolling our tongues together. Biting her lips and she to mine, tasting our blood mixing. I didn't think my dick could get any harder, but here we are.

She brushes my lips with hers. "The wrong side of the tracks." She muses and grins so big I feel an ache in my empty chest.

"You may have started out there, baby. But you are on the right ones now." I dip my hand down between her thighs and enter her again with force. She is so fucking wet for me it takes nothing to allow my fingers back inside of her. Her eyebrows furrowed, and her mouth made an O shape. My girl loves sucking cock based on the amount of natural lube I have in my possession.

I pump harder and start to roll her clit with my thumb. She shatters around me, screaming my name. I pulled out and pushed my fingers into her mouth.

"Take it, baby. Taste what I do to you." And she does. She licks and sucks, and I feel I could fucking come just by watching her devour my fingers.

I aim my cock up against her and slide right in like it was custom fucking made for me.

Fuck, she is tight and clenches around me again. Her body stiffens, and she cries out, leaning her head back. I grab ahold of her throat and squeeze as I pound into her. Her legs wrap around me, and I can tell she is about to come again.

Just before she does, though, I hold my thrusts. She groans like the little furious kitten she can be, and I laugh. "You are so mean, Lincoln!"

You have no idea, baby.

I chuckle, "You have to wait, baby, till I tell you can come."

She pulls me into her more and tries to rub her clit up and down against my stomach. I pull back, sitting up on my knees. She sighs again. I laugh a little harder now. She is so fucking adorable with her sneakiness.

I pull out and flip her over so she is on her tummy. I smack her ass hard, and she whimpers.

"Up," I demand.

She obliges by getting on all fours. I lined up again at her entrance and waited. I have to admire her ass as she pushes up against me. I smack her again and again and again till I start to see my red handprint popping up. She moans with each slap. I line up my dick and thrust hard.

I will make sure she can't sit tomorrow without thinking about me. I fucking own her now.

Then, I think about that fucker Nick and imagine him with his hands on her, and I grow feral. I grab her head with my fist and pull it up. She cries out in pain, but I feel her squeeze my dick like a fucking vice.

"Who do you belong to, Allie?"

She tries to gain her breath since I am pulling her back to me so hard she finds it difficult to breathe.

"Who owns you, baby?" I kiss the side of her face and lick up the tears falling down her precious cheek. I move slowly into her so I can get the answer I want.

She growls and says, "You do."

Damn right I do.

I slam into her. And then grabbed her throat with my other hand. Fisting her hair and tightening my hand around her throat. I feel her getting close. "Good girl. Come for me."

As soon as I say the words, she comes undone. I can't hold it together anymore either and release into her. Putting all my weight down onto her and sinking into the bed. I continue to attack my pussy until there is nothing left. She has milked me till there is nothing more to give.

I rolled off her and pulled her towards me. I place her head on my chest and caress her side with my fingers. She shivers under my care, so I grab the sheet next to us and wrap her up in it.

I kiss the side of her head. She starts to sink into me more and more, with her breathing slowing.

"You are all mine now."

She grunts softly before I feel her body give up the fight. I pulled her closer to me and let her drift deeper into sleep.

Allie

When I open my eyes, I forget where I am for a moment.

There are black sheets all around me, and the large windows are now open. I sit up and remember that I must have slept in Lincoln's bed after we fucked.

Oh god…I fucked him.

Yep…that happened.

Shit.

I got up and saw that I was wearing his t-shirt from last night. Wait, where are my panties? I get up to look around but don't see anything.

Fuck…think I left my purse downstairs too. Wait, did I leave it in the bathroom? Everything seems like a blur…I did take Xanax, so that could be the cause for my forgetfulness. Or the multiple orgasms I received from Lincoln Reynolds.

I go into the bathroom that is attached to the bedroom and find the same aesthetics. Black and even more black. Black tiles with black marble-looking countertops. It all looks very fancy.

I sit down to pee, thinking about last night. Oh god, I told Lincoln that I was his. I place my head in my hands.

I mean, I get it...some guys like to hear that sort of thing during sex, but man, he was for real holding back orgasms. That is taking things a little far, right?

I finish up and go to wash my hands. I look at myself in the mirror for the first time since yesterday. Damn, I look like I got fucked and fucked well. Which, of course, I did.

God, my life is a mess. I need to find Lincoln, get my clothes, find my phone, and get the hell out of here.

I come out of the bedroom quietly since I don't want to run into any parents or anyone else for that matter. Lincoln's shirt is long but it's not that long for me to feel comfortable walking around this huge house in the daylight in nothing else. I let out a heavy sigh.

I decide to go looking for him or clothes. I keep walking till I hear sounds coming from the kitchen.

"Oh! Hello there." A friendly voice calls out as I round the corner.

"Hello," I say meekly.

"Would you like some breakfast, young lady? Mr. Lincoln didn't know what you would want, so he had me make the entire menu for you."

A small, framed woman appears with her salt and peppered hair in a tight bun. She wears an apron and smiles sweetly at me. She looks and acts what I suspect a grandma would act like. I wouldn't know since I never had one.

I look over to the countertop to see an array of food. Pancakes, waffles, bagels, cereal, fruit, muffins, some sort of flat pancake looking thing with cream cheese. Eggs, bacon, sausage…

"Umm, I don't know what to say. You really didn't have to make all this food. It'll just go to waste."

"Oh, honey. Don't you worry about that. Now, sit and eat. What would you like to drink? I could get you some freshly squeezed orange, watermelon, or grapefruit juice."

What in the world?

"No, thank you. Coffee will be fine."

"Cream, sugar, milk, nonfat-"

"Just black is fine," I interrupt her more aggressively than I would have preferred. I smile gently and start to gather a pile on my plate. I have never seen so many different types of breakfast foods in one place, and I am going to eat till I can't walk anymore.

The nice lady comes over, drops off my cup of black coffee, and smiles again. "I am so sorry…what is your name?"

"Ms. Fields, sweetheart."

"Well, thank you, Ms. Fields. This is delicious." I tell her with a mouthful.

"Oh, you are so welcome. Enjoy. I will be leaving soon but Mr. Lincoln said for me to tell you to stay here till he gets back."

"Do you happen to know where he went or how long till he is back?"

"I don't, sweetheart. But please, make yourself at home." And then she is off to grab her purse and things to head out.

Just like that…I am alone and don't know what to do.

I finish my breakfast and wash my dishes. Not certain what to do with the remainder of the food. I try to put some of the stuff that will spoil away in the fridge but there isn't much room there. It seems that each cabinet or drawer is filled with kitchen gadgets or more food.

I tell myself to stuff my purse full of food before I head home. I could eat on some of this stuff for days. I head back towards Lincoln's room and find my clothes have been folded and laid out on the made bed.

Huh, where did those come from?

I walk over and pick them up, getting a smell of detergent. Mmm, it smells so good. I barely get a chance to take my stuff to the laundry these days, and usually, I just wash my shit in the sink with some dishwashing soap. These smell heavenly!

I pull off Lincoln's shirt and start to get dressed. Then I realized that my underwear and jacket were missing. Well, that isn't strange at all, I sigh. God, did Lincoln do something with them? I hope he isn't the type to hold onto a girl's panties he just fucked. I shake off an ick feeling.

I look around for something to throw on since my arms are bare, and I get chilly. I see a black hoodie draped over the chair Lincoln had sat in earlier. It's a Yaverson College hoodie. I decided I would wear it and Lincoln wouldn't mind. And if he does, I can just make it up to him by sucking his huge cock again.

God, Allie, quit thinking of Lincoln's perfect cock.

I put on my boots and headed back downstairs. I don't want to snoop too much, but maybe I can at least find my purse. I walk through the house again and finally find my bag on the counter in the main living room. I rush over and grab my phone to see any messages or missed calls.

Hmm, that is weird. I thought I would have at least heard from Nick. He looked disappointed when he left yesterday. Also, I wonder how Stephanie is doing. I haven't heard from her in a couple of weeks since she told me what happened between her and Brett. I told her to take some time off from working at the bookstore to get better.

It still infuriates me to think about what he did to her. No one deserves the shit he pulled on her, and I wanted to be damn sure he knew it didn't get overlooked.

I start to write out a text to check in on her when I hear a door close behind me. I swiftly turned around and almost dropped my phone from the scare.

Lincoln stands there like a statue. He wore his normal attire: dark blue jeans, a black T-shirt, and black boots. But today, he is wearing a white baseball cap turned backward. I can see strands of his dark hair sticking out on the sides. Just when I think he couldn't get any hotter, he shows up like this.

"Hey there." He strolls over to me with a grin on his face. I feel the wings of butterflies fluttering in my stomach. I can't help the smile that crosses my face and the gush that drips in my shorts.

"God, you scared me." I smack his chest playfully when he comes to stand in front of me. I stand up on my tippy toes so I can throw my arms around his neck and lay my lips on his soft ones. He dips down to meet me and lays his hands on my ass. He squeezes it tightly, lifting me up to meet his body and then drops me back down to earth.

I can feel his hardness pushing into my stomach again, and he groans. I pull on his bottom lip until it pops back. I lick his mouth, and his tongue dives into mine. My head is swimming again, and my pussy clenches. I feel a wetness pool and yearn for his touch.

He pulls back, leaning his head on mine. "Damn, baby, I just want to be inside you all day and night." I giggle, thinking he is fucking crazy to be saying these things to me. I am nothing in this world of his. I am a mere flicker of a flame in this grandiose fireplace of his.

"You are nuts," I tell him, laughing and throwing my head back so I can stare into his eyes that I love so much.

His eyes squint at the sides as he says, "You have no idea." He kisses my forehead and finally releases my ass. "Come with me. I have another surprise for you." He grins.

His fingers intertwine with mine as he starts to lead me out of the room.

"Oh wait," I pull back. "I need to text Stephanie and check in with her."

"Who is Stephanie?" he asks curiously.

"She is a friend of mine. She works with me at the bookstore. I have been covering for her for a couple of weeks now, but she is supposed to start back again tomorrow. I just wanted to see how she was feeling."

I unlocked my phone and searched for her name under messages. Funny, I could have sworn I had one saved already. Anyways, I start a new message and send it out. "Done." Then, I looked up at Lincoln as I threw my arms around his neck.

"Now. Where were you planning to take me before I so rudely interrupted you?" I sigh, tilting my head to the side. His hand lifts my chin to look up.

"I forgive you this time." He kisses my nose and then proceeds to lead me through the house.

I follow Lincoln out the back door and through the backyard. We walked past a house that I had no idea had a pool attached to it. I assume this is what rich folks would refer to as a 'pool house.' The place was a small house!

Damn, I could get used to living like this every day.

It does make me wonder about Lincoln, though. When you have everything you ever wanted handed to you, then where is the fun in getting it? Where is the excitement or the build-up of finally being able to enjoy the one thing you couldn't stop thinking about? I will have to bring it up sometime when he isn't taking me to a place he deems as a surprise.

By the way, I'm not a big fan of surprises.

I never really got any good ones growing up, so most of them have been the bad ones. Such as, surprise Allie guess who came back to live with us? Or surprise Allie, I got you a work permit so now you can go get a job and help us out around here?

The only good surprise I had was when the school said that I could graduate early based on all my extra credits. That was a great day. Speaking of great days...the weather is beautiful, and I love being engulfed in Lincoln's hoodie. I am not sure what the fabric is, but it feels light and super soft.

I lift it up to smell the collar as Lincoln pulls me into the side door. "Were you just smelling my hoodie?" He smiles, and I am busted.

"What? I like the way you smell, ok?" I say sheepishly. He shakes his head from side to side.

I am just enjoying whatever this is for now. Soon it will be over. I mean, considering we had sex, I would be out of his system. I threw my hair up into a messy bun and continued to follow him. He brings me into the house and through some rooms. He takes me to a door that leads downward.

It's not till we get all the way down that I realize it looks to be a basement but with a long corridor. There are doors along the sides, and it's not lit very well. "Where are we?" I ask but get ignored.

Lincoln continues to pull me down to the last door on the right. He looks at me and grins… "Your surprise."

He knocks two times, and the door opens. The blonde-haired guy from the other night stands to the side so we can walk through.

I walk inside and lose my breath, but this isn't a good loss of breath like when you see your high school crush. No, this is a loss of breath, like you just got a gun pulled on you in a dark ally.

I see a metal chair that has been bolted down to the floor. The room is large but empty except for a long metal table that runs along the far wall. There are some cabinets and a sink. What the fuck is this place?

I look to see a body slumped over, sitting on a chair. His hands look like they are tied or cuffed behind his back. His shirt is soaked in blood, and he looks to be struggling for air. I see the guy from the other night, the big one that pulled me off of Brett. He comes up to stand beside this poor soul. He grabs his hair and pulls him back to where I finally get a look at his face.

Holy shit.

Its Brett.

"I told you I would take care of it." Lincoln's voice at the back of my neck pulls me out of my shock. He pulls a chair from the back corner and swings it around to sit backward on it.

He gets right in front of Brett and asks him, "So what are you going to do about Allie here, Brett, hmm? Are you going to call the cops or tell your daddy about what happened the other night?"

Brett's eyes slowly open, and he looks at me with disgust. "Fuck this bitch and her virgin cunt friend. I fucking loved every minute of being in her tight little hole. Her virgin blood was better than any lube you could buy. And I don't care what that little bitch said. She loved every fucking minute of my big dick being inside of her."

Lincoln stands up and punches Brett across the face with a crunch. Blood comes shooting out everywhere, and Brett cries like a baby.

"What a pussy." Lincoln claims as he wipes the blood off his hands with his pants. "Babe."

It takes me a minute to realize that Lincoln is talking to me. "You want to do anything else to him before we let him go?" He asks me nonchalantly.

I look over at Lincoln with confusion. Did he just offer Brett up to me on a platter? This has to be a test...or a joke. "What?" I don't recognize my own voice as it leaves my body.

Lincoln crosses towards me, and for the first time since I met him, I am legitametly afraid. But I can't move; I am frozen in my spot. I knew something wasn't right, but my body betrayed me. She wanted this, and now here we are.

He takes my face in his large hands and looks at me with care in his blue eyes. "We don't want to kill him, but you can do whatever you want." He kisses my nose, and I blink.

"Fuck you, Allie!" Brett spits loudly at me from behind Lincoln. "I knew you were a whore but didn't think you would stoop so low as to fuck a Reynolds to do your dirty work." He laughs. "It makes perfect fucking sense though, considering where you came from, though, no?" He winks.

I dig my nails into my palms and try to calm myself down but fuck this and fuck him.

I walk over to the cabinets and drawers, looking for something specific. I find exactly what I am looking for when I come across a large hunting knife. Yes, this looks like it will do the job.

I turn to the larger guy in the room and ask for his help. "Could you please lift up his shirt?" I smile.

The big dude looks to Lincoln before proceeding. Only when Lincoln gives him a nod does he assist. "What the fuck do you think you are doing, Allie?" Brett questions, and I hear a little nervousness in his voice. Could little ol' me have that effect on him? My inner self is jumping up and down with joy.

"Don't worry, Brett. This will only hurt for a minute." Then I dig the knife into his back, and I start to carve the initials.

I don't know how much time has passed. Once I am finished, I stand back and look at my beautiful artwork. I think Brett fainted a while back. Somewhere between 'a' and 'rapist'. I wish I could take a picture, but I will just have to settle for a mental one.

I put both of my hands in the shape of an L and put them together so they resemble a lens. I make a clicking sound with my mouth and wink with my left eye.

I don't even realize I am smiling till I hear Lincoln's low chuckle from across the room. I look up to meet his stare. I see the admiration in his dark eyes. I see the heated look and only break away from it when I hear Brett grunt. He seems to be waking up now.

I am pulled out of my daze and realize what I just did. My hands are covered in blood, and I just wrote "I am a rapist" on the back of Brett's back. What the fuck have I done?

Lincoln

God. Damn. And. Fuck. Me.

I never believed in love, but after witnessing Allie carve out her revenge and stand there with her hands covered in blood, I must say I get it now.

I understand how you can fall so deep into something that logic doesn't understand it. Your mind just knows that there is nothing that will ever come close to this feeling ever again. No drugs, no amount of violence, no amount of blood, money, or power...you can have all of it if I can have her. I am in fucking love.

I need to keep her forever. I need to make sure she is protected and safe. But, most importantly, I need every motherfucker to know she is mine.

I tell Derek to clean up the mess and Tyler to take fuck face back to where he found him. I have plans for my girl, and it doesn't involve my boys.

I grabbed Allie and led her out of the basement. We keep the rooms down there for torturing, killing, foreplay, parties, or whatever the fuck we want, really.

After I got her back inside the main house and up the stairs, I think she was still not aware of her surroundings. I saw the look of horror on her face as she realized what she had just done. I know that look. It was the same one I had when I killed for the first time.

My father held the knife out to me and said, "Now it's ok, son, just dig it into the side of his neck and pull it out. That's it, and it's all over. Simple."

The man twisted and tried to pull on his restraints, mumbling against the tape across his mouth. I didn't know who the man was, just that he was the father of one of my friends who came to my birthday party.

I didn't know what the man had done. I didn't know why my father specifically wanted him killed, and I didn't even know how to process what my father just asked me to do. Is this why my mother committed suicide? Had he always been like this?

"Go on, Lincoln. Claim your destiny. You are a Reynolds. This is the first step in instilling fear against your enemies." The man tries to scream and gives one last final fight. I assess my feelings...my heart rate is steady, my hands aren't trembling, and my mind is free of anything that could hold me back.

"Lincoln," My dad lays his hand on my shoulder and squeezes. "Don't worry. We all have our first times." He smiles and ushers me towards the sorry bastard.

I nod and stalk forward to stand in front of this groveling man. He is sweaty and bloody. He smells of piss. My lip smirks up in disgust. I take one final look into his eyes before I stab. My right-hand flies up and jabs in the side of his neck.

His eyes bulge out in shock. I pulled the knife out.

That was surprisingly easy.

The blood starts pouring and spurting out all around him. He slumps forward.

That's it.

I guess his soul left his body at some point. I felt lost for a moment and finally realized what I had done. I just killed someone. For a fleeting moment, I feel a rush of guilt come over me. I started to panic, but then I felt my father's hand patting me on the back.

"That's my good boy. Nicely done, son. I am proud of you. Just so you know, this man took our trust for granted. He stole from us, Lincoln, and then attempted to blackmail us. He was a traitor and disrespected our name and family. What you did tonight was right. He deserved it, and his death will be a warning to anyone who wants to fuck with us."

Now that I look at Allie, I can tell her mind is somewhere else, somewhere dark, as she sliced into his flesh. I can smell his blood from where I stand, and my dick keeps getting harder and harder and harder. If my boys had not been there, I would have taken her then. I would have pulled her shorts down and fucked her up against the wall while fuck face heard every fucking moan.

I knew then that she was it for me. Seeing her in her element. Fuck everything else.

This was my motherfucking Queen.

"Are you ok, baby?" I asked her as I led her back into the bedroom. It's early afternoon now, and I have already sent everyone away for the remainder of the weekend. She lets go of my hand only to turn and stare into my eyes. Those green emeralds look back at me, and for some reason, I feel uneasy.

This girl has made me lose all control. I would do anything for her...except let her go, of course.

"I need to go home."

Yeah, Fuck that.

"What are you talking about?" I smile, trying to ease her worry.

I run my hands up and down her arms. She is wearing my hoodie, and it looks fucking good on her. Her hair is up in a messy bun, and she has blood splattered on her face. It's not a lot like when this angel first fell into my arms. No, these are tiny speckles, but I can still see them there.

Her hands are covered. And look at that, my most favorite shade of red.

"Why don't you take a shower first." I look down, silently reminding her that she has blood on her hands.

"Come on." I gently interlace my fingers with hers and head towards my bathroom. I go to the shower and turn it on to start to get hot. She stands in the middle of the room like a little lost doe. The blood from her hands transferred onto mine, so everywhere I touch her, I leave traces. I walk up to her and tilt her head with my fingers.

I can tell that she is starting to regret what she did to Brett, and perhaps she is starting to discover who I truly am. She said at the restaurant that she wanted me to tell her the truth always.

"Hey... it's ok, baby. He deserved every fucking thing that was coming to him. You did nothing wrong." I cup her delicate face and lean down to kiss her. Her body goes limp, and I pull her in closer to me. The blood that covered my hands now covers her round cheeks, and my dick is hard as a motherfucking rock.

I put both hands down and palm her ass hard. She gasps into my mouth and fists my shirt to steady herself.

Don't worry, baby, I got you.

"Lincoln?"

"Mhmm," I murmur.

"I really need to get home." She whispers, trying to catch her breath. "I can shower at home."

I take a deep inhale, calming my racing heart. It's right then that I get the sweet scent of her arousal filling my nostrils, as if the devil himself was sending me a direct message from hell.

My dick strains painfully against my jeans. Fuck…I need to be inside her. I need to remind her who is running this show.

Cupping her face again, I took a moment to search her eyes. Those green pleading eyes stare back at me, waiting for my reply. I take a deep breath and let it feather lightly over her red lips.

"Baby…you are home."

She stiffens. Unsure of what to say and how to approach me, my girl takes a deep breath.

"Please," she begs. "Please, Lincoln, just let me go. I promise I won't tell anyone. I am just as much to blame now, and I promise you can trust me. I won't say anything to anyone." I see the vulnerable tears start to well up at the corners of her eyes.

God

Damn

This is the first time her tears have been from pain and fear, not pain and pleasure. And that shit brings out something deep down I didn't know I had in me still.

"Beg me again," I whisper harshly.

Her eyebrows furrow in confusion. "What?"

I spin her around and push her front up against the counter. She squeals at my sudden harsh movements. Pushing into her so hard, I am sure she'll have bruises on her pelvic bones. I grab ahold of her throat and feel her pulse beating fast. It occurs to me then that her throat is a perfect fucking fit for my hand. She looks up at me. Her eyes widened.

I lean down and whisper into her ear. "I said…beg me again. Tell me how you don't want to get me in trouble. Tell me what a good girl you will be for me." I kiss her lightly on the cheek as I squeeze a little more around her neck. I push my hard as fuck dick into her back.

As if I pushed a secret button to unlock a hidden world, her ass can't help but push back into me. I groan as she whimpers.

"Please." Her eyes are closed now.

No, we can't have that.

"Open your eyes," I command.

She doesn't open her eyes, and I see the tears start to flow. I take my free hand that was holding her against the counter up to fist her hair and pull back hard. "I said, open your eyes."

She cries out the loudest I have ever heard her, and it's as if a beautiful songbird just flew into my life. She opens her eyes and looks at herself. Her whimpers have become louder. My dick is so hard I feel I could hammer in a fucking nail.

She doesn't want to see how beautiful she is…fine, I will fucking show her.

"You are so fucking beautiful, Allie." I let go of her but keep her pinned with my body.

I grab the bottom of my hoodie along with her shirt and pull it straight up and off. I give myself an imaginary pat on the back for deciding to throw out all of Allie's underwear. She doesn't need them anymore.

Shorts are the next to go, but I can't keep my fingers out of her for another second. I push my hand down into the front of her shorts.

She protests and tries to stop me, but I am too strong for her. She claws and scratches like my ferocious kitten.

I make it to my pussy faster than she can do any real damage to my arm. She cries harder as I find what I knew I would...she is fucking soaked. I can't help but laugh.

"Awe, there she is." I sink into her neck and bite down. She clenches around my fingers as I stroke in and out of her slowly. "God damn. I don't think my cup will ever be filled by you, Allie. I will always want more."

"Please, Lincoln. Please don't do this. Please...stop," she begs. I continue to push inside of her deeper and deeper. Faster and faster.

"Awe, baby. Are you sure you want me to stop?" I increase my speed, knowing how close she is. Her tears are falling even heavier now.

"Yes...yes, please stop." I love her tenacity, but her breaths are becoming more labored now. She is losing this fight with herself.

"Fuuuuck. I love it when you beg. Tell me again, baby, what do you want? I don't think I got it quite right the first time?" I kiss lightly on her neck. "Do you want me to stop, huh?" As soon as she reaches the edge, I fist her head harder and say into her ear, "that's my good girl."

She crashes into my arms and screams out my name. Her entire body stiffens for two beats, and then she falls limply into my arms. I catch her as she comes down. I lean her head back and pull her chin up with my slippery fingers that house her arousal. I want my earned vulnerability from her. I want those walls broken and everything burned on the inside. Her soul is mine...just as much as mine is hers.

"Who do you belong to?" I whisper while I run my wet thumb over her bottom lip. And fuck me, she must have bitten her lip at some point. Her lips glisten with her natural arousal and blood.

I glance back up into those brilliant emeralds with blown pupils. She slowly opens her eyes and searches within mine. I see her fight leave her body and watch as she accepts her fate.

"You." She blinks, and two tears fall down her flushed cheeks.

Damn right, I do.

They say God works in mysterious ways. You want to know what I think? I think God is a sadistic motherfucker.

These are the thoughts that run through my mind as I look into Lincoln's eyes as he holds my head after giving me the most intense orgasm of my entire life. So yeah, God and I are not on good terms right now.

If he works in mysterious ways, I guess this is why he has made me the perfect toy for Lincoln Hamilton Reynolds III. The boy who can get whatever he wants, when he wants...now he wants me. I am fucked. Literally and metaphorically.

I look into his handsome eyes, and suddenly, my body craves another orgasm. She is a traitorous bitch.

"I love you." He says, looking down at me as he gently strokes my cheek.

I am still trying to catch my breath from all the adrenaline that has coursed through my body. God he is handsome, and I don't know what to do. I am also trying to process what the fuck he just told me.

He lets go of me, seeming to not need a response, removes my shorts, and picks me up bridle style. He carries me to the shower and places me on the bench seat. He steps outside of the shower and removes all his clothing.

This is the first time in the full light that I get to see Lincoln without any clothes on. If God did intend for me to be Lincoln's toy, then he at least gave me the courtesy by making him fucking hot as hell. My clit betrays me again by making me fully aware of her presence.

Yeah, yeah, I know, clit, you are a greedy bitch.

He walks in, and the water starts to fall, running down his muscular chest. I see what his tattoo is around his torso. It's all black and grey. It's an angel falling as if it was pushed off the side of a building, knowing full well who pushed it toward its demise. The left-wing is burning, engulfed in flames. The wing closest to Lincoln's hip is burning too, but beneath the flames, you can see a bat wing emerge. It's as if the angel is eerily transforming into a beast as it falls into the pits of hell.

It's beautiful.

Soap suds start to roll down the tattoo, and I am pulled out of my trance. Lincoln stands in front of me and stroking his hard length. He eyes me up and down as he strokes his hard cock, and my pussy clenches. I whine, wanting his hands on me again. My eyes shut and then I feel him grab the back of my head.

His intimidating form hovers over me, indicating what he really wants from me. I know I am in this now, and the only way out is through. I look into his dark eyes and get to my knees. He shoves his dick into my mouth, and I instinctively moan.

Lincoln throws his head back, and I start to pump his cock with my hand as I bob my head up and down. My jaw hurts, and my throat's aching. He pushes deeper and deeper into the back of my mouth. Each time my pussy betrays me by clenching over and over.

He holds me down for a moment, and I honestly feel like I will pass the fuck out, but right before I do, he pulls out. I cough and gag from the forcefulness.

"Fuuuck, Allie."

I squint and blink, trying to regain my vision. The water is now dripping down my wet hair and into my face. I watch as the droplets sink below me, swirling down the drain. Lincoln kneels beside me. He grabs the back of my head, pulling me to stare at him again.

"Stick out your tongue, beautiful." And I do.

He runs his hand down my face and spits in my mouth. I close my mouth, swallow, and stick my tongue out again for his viewing pleasure.

"Fuck...You're such a good girl aren't you Allie?" He looks down at me with his beautiful blue eyes. I smile, without thought, because my body wants to absorb every glorious drop of his praise.

"Come on, baby."

He stands me up, washes my hair, cleans me with soap that claims to smells like white sandy beaches, and turns off the shower. He takes a soft, fluffy white towel from the cabinet and starts to dry me off. It's a softness I am not used to. I wonder how much these towels cost…I bet they would cover my water bill for a month.

Once we are both dry, Lincoln grabs my wrist and drags me back to the bedroom. The sun appears to be setting soon. Fuck…how long have I been here? Shit, where is my phone?

"Come here, baby."

Lincoln tells me to lay down on the bed and spread my legs. My body moves on autopilot.

He climbs up and lands between my legs. He is holding himself up, and his dark brown hair falls from his face. Droplets start to land on my naked body, but then he lowers himself to kiss me.

He starts slow, but then it becomes savage. He puts his hands on both sides of my head and pulls it from side to side to put it where he wants it. He dominates my mouth; when he growls, I moan. It's the most beautiful sound I have ever heard. I can't help but wrap my legs around his waist, even though he didn't tell me to.

I can't keep my hands off him. I drag my nails down his back in protest. Fuck him for making me feel this way. He fists my hair in retaliation, and we go back and forth like this until he can't take it anymore.

He pulls back and rests on his knees between my legs. He starts to run his tongue down my throat and then grabs ahold of my tit. He squeezes hard and then takes my nipple into his wet mouth. He licks, sucks, and bites me till I can't help but rub my eager clit on his stomach. He laughs and then proceeds to drop lower till I feel his breath on my folds.

I close my eyes wanting to just drown in this moment for now. I know I should leave. I know I should get the hell out of here as quickly as possible, but my body wants him. My body wants Lincoln.

He inhales my pussy and says, "God damn, Allie you smell fucking amazing." Then he licks me from the bottom up. His wet tongue flattens, and I feel him everywhere. His hands have tightened around my legs, and he digs his fingers into my thighs. I feel the bruises starting to build, and it makes me clench my pussy even more.

He licks my clit expertly and slowly. "Please, Lincoln. Don't tease me. I can't take it anymore." He laughs and then digs his fingers deeper into my flesh.

"Awe, baby. Don't worry. I know what you need." He drives three fingers into me faster and harder. He licks and sucks on my clit till I feel my body stiffen. "Fuck. I could taste your juices for the rest of my life." He takes a big inhale as he continues to drive his fingers into me, demanding my attention. He takes another inhale before he eats my pussy like a starved man. I feel like the smell has awakened something inside of him because he is no longer the calm, collected, mysterious boy he usually is.

Now, he has become an animal. I can't hold on longer, and my body is craving a release. I want to feel good again. I just want to forget all the bad and feel something good

"Eyes on me, Allie, as I make you come with my mouth." I look down at Lincoln as he eats me out like I am his last meal. He takes his hand that was holding my leg down and squeezes my tit. He is still attacking my pussy with his fingers and tongue. I feel I am about to come as I look into his eyes. My body is so tight I pray for the release I now know that only he can give me.

He slaps my breast so hard that I clench again, and then I let it all go. I jumped off the cliff and fell into the ecstasy that he held over my head. My heart rate is speeding as I try to catch my breath. I close my eyes and barely register that Lincoln has climbed up my body and now lies between my legs again.

He grabs my jaw with his wet hands and pulls my face to look at him. I lazily open my eyes. I can see the proof of my orgasm all over his handsome face.

I am his prey. I am his toy. I am his.

He crashes his mouth onto mine, and I can see fucking stars behind my eyes. I smell myself in his mouth and feel the wetness on my nose and cheeks from his hand.

He pulls his mouth away only to drive his fingers into my mouth.

"Lick me clean, baby," he demands.

And I do.

I lick his fingers and pull them into my mouth. He pushes them so far back into my throat that I gag. I feel the tears starting to form in the corners of my eyes. I feel his large, long fingers dive deeper into the back of my throat. I choke and cough while trying to breathe through my nose. "That's my good fucking girl."

He pulls out his fingers as I try to gain some air again. I don't get a chance for long before I feel him enter me.

He slams inside me without permission.

He slams inside me without remorse.

He slams inside me without empathy.

Last night, I was on my stomach, so I didn't get to see Lincoln lose himself inside of me. Seeing him like this wasn't what I was expecting. I am getting lost in his pleasure as he pounds into me more and more. He bends down to ravage my neck as if he is pissing on his territory.

He groans and pushes deeper and deeper. I am reaching my climax, but before I do, I pull his head up to look into his eyes. If he wanted my vulnerability, then motherfucker, you best believe I was stealing his.

"Are you going to come for me, baby?" He asks me, but I know he means it as giving me permission.

"Yes." I nodded, and then I screamed his name for what felt like the hundredth time.

I watch as his orgasm engulfs him fully, and he rides the wave onto shore with me. He lost that side of him that I saw earlier. Now, all I see is a broken boy. Maybe he and I are just broken together. Maybe I should stop fighting to be his and accept it. Not sure what that all entails but let's just ride it out and see together.

I decide to give this, whatever the fuck this is, a try just as Lincoln comes up to clean me up. He came inside me twice now with no condoms. I am on the shot, so not concerned with pregnancy, but I should probably find out if he has anything else that I should be worried about.

"Um, can I ask you something?"

Lincoln's eyebrows furrow. "Sure, babe. You can ask me anything."

"So, I know you have been with a lot of girls. Or I mean, from your reputation, or from what I have heard anyways--"

"Just spit it out, Allie. You don't ever need to hide from me. What is it?"

"Do I need to get tested?" Not expecting that question, he bursts out in laughter. I have never seen this side of him before. He laughs so hard that it makes me start to laugh. I kick him off the bed just as he is getting up to grab the blanket to cover our bodies with. He drops down beside me in this soft, comfy bed.

"It's not funny. Why are you laughing at me?" I pout by sticking out my bottom lip. His gaze gets heated.

"What?" I ask concerned.

"Oh, nothing. You just have a little cut on your bottom lip." He lays down and pulls me into him close.

I touch my bottom lip and feel a bump. He kisses my forehead as I snuggle into his side. He is wearing white boxer briefs again, like the ones I saw before. God, he is so hot.

"So yeah, do I need to get tested or what, Lincoln?" I huff.

"No. Damn. No, you don't need to get tested. I never fucked anyone without a condom before you. You're good."

His announcement sends my head in a spiral. "Never?" I asked, perplexed.

He turns me over to spoon me from behind and nestles his nose in the back of my head. It sends a shiver straight to my core. "No, baby. Never. I told you. I'm yours as much as you are mine."

I close my eyes and take in the warm embrace that I feel blanketing around me. Just as I am about to settle in, I feel Lincoln shift and pick up something from the nightstand. He pulls my unruly blonde strands away from my neck and leans in to kiss the sweet spot between my neck and shoulder. I sigh with a small smile on my face and rest my head further on the pillow below my heavy head. It's then that I hear the click of a picture being taken.

I open my eyes to find Lincoln staring back at me through selfie mode on his phone. You can see his blue eyes staring back, just above my neck, and his dark hair hanging over his forehead.

My serene and content face is in clear view. He closes the phone and drops it to the floor without moving.

"Go to sleep, baby. Tomorrow is a new day."

I shudder to think what tomorrow will bring since I am essentially a prisoner here. I take a deep inhale and smell the floral scent I now know so well. I tell myself not to get used to this feeling right now because I am certain it will be out of his system soon.

Lincoln

"Did you get everything I asked for?" I ask Mrs. Fields as I finish up my second cup of coffee.

"Yes, sir, Mr. Lincoln, sir. I made sure I got an assortment of different styles of clothing for Ms. Allie. I went off the sizes you gave me, but if anything doesn't fit, I will be happy to return."

"Good." I stand up and stroll down the hallway away from the kitchen. I need to go wake up my girl because if not, she will be late for school.

When I walk into the dark bedroom, I can hear the sweet little noises her nose makes when she sleeps. I wish I could crawl in bed with her and worship her body more, but that will have to come later.

"Allie," I whisper over her beautiful face and plant a small kiss on her smooth cheek. She grunts and rolls over away from me. I laugh at her attempt to get rid of me. "Come on, baby, you're going to be late for school. I will give you a ride." At hearing that, she springs up from the bed in one quick movement. The comforter falls from her naked body, and I see her hard, pebbled nipples begging to be played with. I grab my dick to ease the ache, but it just makes it worse.

Unluckily for me, she is out of bed and running into the bathroom before I hold her down and pound my cock into her eager pussy.

"I don't have any clothes, Lincoln! How am I supposed to go to school?" I hear her yell over the sound of her peeing.

"Mrs. Fields went shopping yesterday for you. You will find a whole bunch of shit in the closet for you to pick from. Anything you don't like, just set it on the bed, and she will handle it." Allie comes out of the bathroom, holding a towel around her body.

"What do you mean she went shopping for me?" She looks at me doe-eyed.

I open the closet door and show her all the outfits she has at her disposal. Her mouth drops, and she gasps. "I will be downstairs. Don't leave me waiting long. I have shit to do after I drop you off." I kiss her head and walk out the door.

I stand at the top of the stairs, pausing before I start my descent. I open my social accounts and post the picture I took last night of both of us and caption it with "mine."

Perfect.

Now every motherfucker knows not to fuck with what's mine.

I look over the entire closet, and I am speechless. I have no words for what I see before me. It's as if I went to bed and woke up a princess. I see tons of dresses, pants, skirts, jeans, shirts, blouses, heels, boots, and belts. I mean, I could keep going, but I think you get the picture. I even see an array of different types of bags, purses, totes, and bookbags.

I looked through the shirts and found one that I like, it's a white shirt with some graffiti art on it. I look for underwear but come up empty-handed. What the fuck is with having no underwear?

I pulled the shirt over my head and found some designer blue jeans. They fit me perfectly, and I grab some socks and some Converse shoes. This will work for today. I also found Lincoln's hoodie and decided to grab that as well in case I get cold.

I headed downstairs and heard Mrs. Fields call out to me. "Oh, hello, sweetheart! I hope you like the clothes I got you. If there is anything you need a different size in, just let me know. Also, if there is something specific you wanted me to get, just jot it down for me, and I can pick it up for you later," she smiles and hands me an apple to take with me.

"Thank you. I really appreciate you doing this for me. Oh! One thing, umm," I whisper now closer to her. "Did you buy me any underwear by any chance?"

Mrs. Fields shrugs it off like I asked her how much I needed to pay for these items, "Oh sweetie, Mr. Lincoln said you wouldn't be needing anything in that department."

She cups my cheek and saunters off back to doing whatever she was doing before I came in.

What just happened?

I glance at the clock on the wall and grab my shit before I am super late to school. I know that Lincoln's car is fast, but not looking to get killed today.

I walk outside and find Lincoln already in the car, waiting for me to get in. I settle down next to him, and he looks over at me with silver aviators. Damn, he is hot in those.

"Ready, babe?" He smiles, and I nod.

"No underwear...really, Lincoln? What the fuck? I need panties and bras!" I yell at him as he pushes the car into gear. I slam against the seat and fidget with my seatbelt.

Lincoln smirks and looks over at me. My pussy likes it, and it makes me aware of her admiration. Damn it, this is why I need panties.

"I like having easy access to what belongs to me. You don't need underwear daily. It's just absurd."

Oh my god, is he for real?

"Absurd! Lincoln, this is not cool. I will need underwear." My voice overpowers the NIN 'We're in This Together' playing from the speakers.

I swear he listens to The Fragile album on repeat.

He laughs, "Ok, fine...I will have Mrs. Fields get you some." He grabs my hand and kisses the back of it. The action is so intimate I am not certain how to feel. This feeling is completely foreign to me.

I tell Lincoln to drop me off a block away from the school so I can walk the rest of the way, but he ignores me and parks right in front of the building. Everyone is staring at the most expensive car to ever pull into Riverdale High.

I already feel the eyes on me as Lincoln gets out on his side. He rounds the car and before I can get out, he is there to help me. "Thank you, but I can manage," I say, trying to get this awkwardness over with sooner rather than later.

I see more and more eyes looking over at us as everyone gathers around. My hands start to sweat, and I can't seem to swallow. I want to tell Lincoln that it was a mistake to bring me and if he could just take me back to his warm, soft, comfortable bed.

I feel his fingers tilt my chin up to meet his eyes. I feel an ease wash over me like he could slay all my demons with one strike.

"Be a good girl today at school. I will be right here to pick you up." He kisses me on the nose and then moves aside for me to walk in. I smile back and move forward to find Stephanie as quickly as possible.

I hear the whispers all around me as I walk past everyone in the halls. I make it to my locker without anyone assaulting me or sneering. I am surprised that not one person has asked me why the fuck Lincoln Reynolds was dropping me off in front of the school, and not only that, but he looked to be intimate with me.

I open my locker and grab my things for the first period since I missed homeroom. I feel a hand on my back and look to see a young girl with brown hair staring up at me.

"Girl...what the fuck was that this morning?" Stephanie asks.

"I know. It's a long story," I said, closing my locker and turning towards her. "How are you feeling?" her smile drops, and I see her uneasiness.

"I am feeling better. Thank you, Allie." I place my hand on her shoulder and tell her that everything will be ok. I honestly don't know if it will, but that is all I can think about right now. I need to continue to focus on my school and try to get out of here as soon as possible.

"Have you seen Nick at all? I haven't spoken to him since Saturday and it's not like him to ignore me." I asked Stephanie.

"Hah! Yeah, you probably won't be hearing from Nick, especially since Lincoln Reynolds basically staked his claim on you this morning."

"What?"

"You didn't check Lincoln's Instagram? Yeah, he posted a photo of you two stating that you were his in a nutshell. I doubt any guy will talk with you for the rest of the year. And the girls will likely want to poison you for taking him off the market."

"Ah fuck," I sigh. Great, just what I needed to happen.

"Yeah, girl. Now, I am curious. How did you manage to get him?"

"I honestly have no fucking clue, Stephanie." We kick off heading to class, and now I see it in the eyes of my schoolmates. Every girl wishes I was dead and no guy would make eye contact. Before, I was invisible, but now, I am but with a big target on my back.

I finish up my classes before lunch without any encounters. It's not till I go to the girl's bathroom that I hear Brittany Benson and her squad come in behind me. Brittany's family lives on the same street as Nick's, which means she is middle class, but she still feels elite towards people like me. She throws her long, blonde hair over her shoulder as she looks at me with disgust.

"What the fuck, Allie? How did someone like you get the attention of someone like Lincoln Reynolds?" She eyes me up and down, I assume, pricing my outfit inside her small, minded head.

Brittany is the most popular girl at our school, and she is the nastiest. One time, she thought a girl was trying to steal her boyfriend. She made the girl suck a guy's dick on the football team and recorded it so she could share it with everyone. The poor girl was mortified because she had never done it before. The bullying got so bad she ended up switching schools mid-year.

I normally flew under her radar, but I guess Lincoln's caveman-like behavior caught her attention. I look at her and her two minions behind her, and honestly, I feel bad.

"Look, Brittany, I don't know what to say. I am sure this thing he has for me is going to go away before you can blink." I wash my hands and throw the brown, flimsy paper napkins into the trash. "If you want, I will put in a good word for you, ok?"

Instead of taking this as an olive branch, she pushes me down onto the dirty floor and hovers above me. "Don't fucking condescend me, Allie. You better talk nicely about me the next time I see you. I will get close to him even if I have to use you in the process. Nice outfit, by the way. You better enjoy the nicer things in life because you don't belong there, Allie. You are trash and always will be trash." She washes her hands and throws her trash in my face. She turns and walks out with her followers following.

The rest of the day goes by in a blur. I wonder what the fuck I am doing with Lincoln. Brittany was right. I should get out now before I get used to having nice things. I decide to tell him that when he picks me up, but when I walk out the school doors at the end of the day, I lost my trail of thoughts.

He is leaning up against the hood of his car, hands in his pockets, wearing his silver aviators, and now he has a white fitted T-shirt with a black backward cap on. Why does he have to be so devilishly handsome? He takes a drag of his cigarette, and instead of stubbing it out on his boot, he flicks it off his thumb and forefinger like before. I sauntered up to him and watched as a lazy smile appeared on his face.

"You know that is littering, Mr. Reynolds?" I tease.

"Oh yeah, well, I guess one man's trash is another man's treasure." He smirks and grabs onto my hips, pulling me into his hard body. The double meaning of his words isn't lost on me. I am trash, but to him, I am treasure. All my awful feminist thoughts have melted away, and I am star-struck. He kisses me lightly on my lips and cups my face.

"Did you have a good day, baby? Learn a lot and shit?" He slaps my ass, indicating I need to move. I decide to ignore Brittany's remarks from before and just try to enjoy whatever this is for the moment. I am sure he will get tired of me within the next week.

"Yeah, I learned tons, in fact! All about possessiveness, and jealousy, and envy, and cavemen-like behavior." I count each observation off on my fingers with a pensive look on my face. "Would you know anything about that?" I ask as I come around to the passenger side door.

His beautiful face smiles, and he runs a thumb over my bottom lip. "I know all about staking a claim if that is what you are insinuating, Allie. And, in my world, staking a claim is necessary." He pulls down my bottom lip till it pops back in place. "Let's go home, baby. I am hungry, and I bet you are too." As if he summoned my stomach with his mind, my tummy growls. He chuckles and then heads out of the school parking lot.

It's been three weeks since Allie has been staying with me, and my father hasn't said one word to me about it. It's for the best because I don't fucking care what his thoughts are on the matter. She is mine, and what is mine stays with me.

We finish eating dinner and go to the theater room to watch TV. We wait for the show to start that Allie picked to watch, and I wonder what the assignment still is that my father wants us to be working on.

I swear, if he doesn't tell us soon, then I am going to start to think there is no fucking assignment, and he is just stringing me along for the fuck of it. He thinks I need to learn the ins and outs of politics so I can go into that when I graduate. He has no clue that I don't plan on following in his footsteps. I plan on making my own empire and won't need his help to do it.

Allie shifts next to me rubbing her leg against mine. I love the heat she radiates off her, and my body can't get enough.

I grab her thigh and squeeze till she turns her head to look at me.

"Lincoln?"

"Yes, baby." I lean over and kiss her temple.

"When are you going to let me go home?" I stiffen.

"Why do you want to go back there?"

She moves to where she can face me and takes a deep inhale. My shirt hangs off the side of her right shoulder, and I see a small bite mark on her collarbone from the other night. I smile internally. Her black leggings are the only thing keeping me from ramming my dick into her tight pussy.

"I don't belong here." She sniffs and looks around the room. I can see the tears welling up in her eyes, and my dick twitches. "I'm not supposed to be here...I mean, don't get me wrong, I love it here and Mrs. Fields and you have been wonderful to me, but I really should be getting back to my home. To where I come from."

Who the fuck has been telling her she doesn't belong?

"You mean the place where no one gives a fuck about you, and you have no future?"

Her look of anger makes my dick even harder. She goes to stand up, but I grab ahold of her arm and slam her ass on my lap.

"Let me go, Lincoln. I don't need you. I was doing fine without you before." She is clawing at me and wants to wrestle to get out of my hold. She has no clue what she has stirred in me.

"Oh, is that right, Allie?" I whispered into her ear. "You don't need me, huh?" I pick her up from her hips and push her down on her tummy so her ass is over my knee.

"Ge the fuck off me, Lincoln! Let me go!" she screams.

I smack her ass hard. She continues to wiggle, trying to get out of my grasp. I smack her ass again. I keep smacking till she stills.

She is quiet now except for the sweet sounds of her sobbing. I pull down her leggings and see the redness from my assault. "Fuck, baby...what you do to me." I rub it soothingly to ease the pain.

"Please. Please, Lincoln." she whimpers.

I push my fingers through her slit and immediately feel the wetness coat my hand. "There she is. Oh, baby, tell me again how you don't need me?"

I push two fingers inside of her and slip in and out of her warm walls. She shivers beneath me. My dick is now painfully hard inside of my jeans.

"Tell me, baby, tell me you don't want me to touch you that you don't need me to touch you and make you come." I keep fingering her with my left hand and take my right to smack her ass again.

Allie's body betrays her, and she tightens around my fingers as I increase my speed. Just as she is about to come, I slow down to hear her grunts of frustration. I chuckled lightly and then returned to my torture.

"Do you want to tell me something now, Allie?" I increase my intensity and roll my thumb over her clit.

This time, she gives me what I want...her obedience. "Yes, Lincoln...oh god, yes, I need you. Please don't stop. Please. Please let me come." I finger her faster and continue to slap her ass till she comes all over my hand.

Her body rides out the wave of euphoria, and I turn her limp body over to lay across my lap. I pull her heavy head up to meet my eyes. Her pupils are dilated, and she is still trying to catch her breath. I run my thumb over her cheek as I cup her face.

"No one tells you where you do and don't belong except for me. And you belong with me." I rub my nose up hers and kiss her. I dominate her mouth so she can't breathe. I pull her into me so she can't fight. I own her.

It's now been two months since I have been living with Lincoln, and tonight is the first night I will be meeting his father. Lincoln was instructed to go to a charity ball that his father is co-hosting, and he is taking me as his date. I have never been to a fancy ball, but Mrs. Fields bought me a beautiful gold sequined dress that fits my small, curvy frame very well. The dress reveals most of my back as it dips about two inches up from my tailbone. There is a small bow tie at my back that rests between my shoulder blades to keep the front taught. Its beautiful.

Mrs. Fields also had someone come in to professionally do my hair and makeup. I look very different than I normally do, and I'm not sure how I feel about it. I stand in front of the long mirror and stare at myself for the 100th time.

"You look stunning," I hear Lincoln behind me and turn. He stands in an all-black tuxedo, and his hair is slicked back. I never see him dressed up like this, and I wish I had panties on since I am pooling now.

"Damn it, Link...you need to let me wear panties again because this is not cool." He laughs loudly and comes to stand behind me, looking at us in the mirror. His warm chest is up against my bare back.

"You look even more like a fucking goddess than you normally do." His words send shivers down my body, and my legs are already giving out on me.

"Stop. It took way too long to get my makeup and hair done. You do not get to ruin it before the night has started." I nudge him from behind, hoping my ass will get him to back off, but instead, it creates a grunt. I thread my fingers through my long blonde hair as it falls down my back. I can see my dark hair is starting to grow out more but I don't mind.

"Baby, when we get back home, I am going to ruin you." He kisses my neck gently.

"Promise." I sigh into him.

"I don't make promises, baby, but I will for you. And yes. It's a fucking promise." I giggle and turn around to meet his handsome face. I throw my arms around his neck as his hands land on my ass.

"Thank you." His eyebrows frown at me in question. "For giving me a night like tonight. I will remember it always."

Lincoln cups my face and kisses me on my nose. "There will be a lot more in your future, kitten." I blink away the tears in my eyes, knowing that what he says is probably not true. I believe this world will chew me up and spit me out, just like everything else that has ever happened to me. But, for tonight, I allow myself to have this.

"I forgot something." Lincoln pulls out a necklace from his pocket and holds it in front of me. It's a beautiful, dainty silver necklace with a heart-shaped emerald. "Oh my god, Link, it's beautiful." He lifts it up to fasten it around my neck.

"Not as beautiful as the girl wearing it." He kisses my neck, takes two steps backwards and puts out his hand for me to take, which I happily do.

"Like that wasn't the cheesiest thing you have ever said?" I roll my eyes at him, and he laughs.

Our black limo pulls up to the mansion and I'm already thankful I had a little Champagne on the way. I have never been to a party like this and never met Lincoln's father so killing two birds of this magnitude with one small stone is giving me anxiety.

Lincoln places his warm hand in mine, and I instantly feel at ease. His presence can make me feel safe, but he can also make me feel hauntingly afraid. He kisses the back of my hand and reiterates how we only must stay for an hour then he can take me home and ruin me.

The evening feels incredibly dark, and the flames from the candles on the exterior flicker in the wind. The butterflies in my stomach won't settle down until I feel Lincoln's warm hand on the small of my back. I look up at his kind eyes tonight.

He ushers me inside, and we wait in line to be introduced to the family hosting this event. Lincoln is on his best behavior, and it's unusual to see him like this. We finish with our greetings and head out to mingle. Lincoln is polite and pleasantly talks to everyone who introduces themselves to him. I stand on his arm and wait till I am asked a question. I am extremely uncomfortable being out of my element, but Lincoln never makes me feel like I don't belong.

It's the girls I go to school with and the glares I get from anyone who meets me. I am not from another elite family, and I didn't inherit money either. I am just a girl who caught the attention of Lincoln Hamilton Reynolds III.

"And this is Lincoln, my son." I hear a booming voice come up from behind us as a man pats Lincoln on the back aggressively. Even if this man hadn't proclaimed his son, I still would have picked him as Lincoln's father. He was tall, slim, and had the same shade of hair Lincoln did.

"Ah, nice to meet you, Lincoln. Your father has told us wonderful things about you." The man standing across from Lincoln said. He was a heavier-set man with gray hair and hairy hands.

"Well, I am sure he embellished most of them," Lincoln quips back, showcasing his beautiful smile.

"Nonsense. Listen, after you graduate, if you want to see how a real political campaign is run you look me up. With your looks and connections, we could easily sway the vote," he muses. "Ah, and who is this lovely lady?" the older man says, looking into my eyes.

"This is Allie Parker. My girlfriend."

I push my hand out to introduce myself. I start to speak to the older man, thanking him for the compliment, but Lincoln's dad cuts me off. I cut my eyes towards him. He looks like I just slit his own mother's throat and made him watch me do it.

"You know, Oliver, let's get another drink, shall we?" and as quickly as they appeared, they disappeared. I take a deep breath, trying to catch my own and then I feel Lincoln by my ear. "Yeah, not sure if you figured it out yet, but my dad is a fucking dick."

I can't help the giggle that comes out of my mouth at Lincoln's opinion of his father. I look up at his blue eyes, and he smiles at me with a care I can't put a name on. It feels like we are the only two people in the room.

"Lincoln!" I hear a shriek and glance over my shoulder. A tall blonde with big boobs comes up and pushes herself into Lincoln hugging him. Lincoln doesn't reciprocate, but that doesn't deter this girl. She continues to eye him up and down and makes small talk with him as if I am not even there.

"Oh my god, it's been so long," she licks her lips seductively. "My father and yours are talking in the grand hall." She takes a sip from her full glass of Champagne and finally looks over to me. Her glance is dismissive.

"Katherine Sinclair, I would like you to meet my girlfriend, Allie Parker." Lincoln lands his hand on my hip and pulls me in closer to him.

Katherine looks down at me with disdain in her eyes. She must have thought I was a date for the evening and nothing more. I can see her eyeing me from head to toe as she takes stock of her competition. I give her my biggest fake smile and stick my hand out for hers.

"It's a pleasure to meet you, Ms. Sinclair." She eyes my hand as if it's covered in shit and dismisses me again.

"Lincoln, could we maybe go somewhere and talk for a moment? In private," she glances my way at this last part.

"Sorry, Katherine. We don't plan on staying long. But it was nice to see you again." He pulls me along in the direction of the bar.

"Who was that?" I ask Lincoln as I look back over my shoulder. If looks could kill, I would be dead.

"She's nobody. Just a friend of the family." Lincoln pulls me over to a hidden spot behind a column in the back and pushes me up against it. My hot body collides with the cold stone, and I let out a gasp from the impact.

"I can't stop thinking about your tight cunt underneath this dress, baby." His blue eyes are dark and hooded as he peers down at me. I smile at the fact I can still influence him like this. Lincoln thrives on being in control, but I won't tell him if you don't.

"Is that so?" I tease.

Lincoln bends down to kiss my neck, and I turn, allowing him to devour me. His hand comes up my thigh, and I open my legs wider for his intrusion. His fingers brush along my folds and I shiver from his touch.

"Lincoln," I whine and bury my head in his shoulder. As soon as his fingers enter me, his phone vibrates. I giggle and ask, "Is that your phone or another surprise for me?" I feel the smile on his face as he laughs into my shoulder.

"Fuck...it's my dad. He is the only one on my list that will get through to me tonight. If it were any other night, I would ignore it, but I must show up if he calls." He pulls out his wet fingers and puts them up to my face.

"Clean me off, baby." I maintain eye contact as I lick his fingers from the bottom all the way to the top. I can taste myself on him, and I groan as his other hand comes up around my throat.

"Let me get this shit over with my dad, and then we'll leave. Go get yourself a glass of something and wait for me." He kisses me softly on the lips and leads me out from the shadows.

I watch Lincoln exit the room down a hallway before I turn to the bartender and order another Champagne. I'm admiring the decorations when I hear her voice again.

"So, how did you get Lincoln Reynolds to bring you to an event like this one?" I slowly turned to see Katherine again. Big boobed, blonde, wearing a low-cut sapphire blue dress and covered in jewels. "Blackmail? Sex?"

"Honestly, I don't know what you are talking about. You heard Lincoln himself. I am his girlfriend." I smile and take a sip from my glass.

"Bullshit. There is something going on here, and I will find out. Or I can just wait it out. He will eventually get tired of you and realize you have nothing to your name." She tilts her head while still taking stock. "You can't provide him with anything that he doesn't already have. You don't belong here, trash, and you never will. God, you can't even afford to have your roots dyed. Pathetic," she huffs with humor. "Besides, his father and mine are talking right now about the arranged marriage proposal. It's only a matter of time now." She smiles, and her perfectly straight, pearly white teeth mock my ignorance.

I stare at her with fury in me because, deep down, I know she is right. I shouldn't be here, and it's just a matter of time before I am kicked out of this lifestyle. I can feel my strength oozing out of my body, and I try to hold back the tears that want to stream out.

"Allie!" I hear Lincoln's demanding voice call me from across the room. His tall, dark figure stands by the front door. He waves me towards him, implying we can leave.

"Enjoy it while it lasts, trailer trash." I hear Katherine tell me as I quickly walk to Lincoln.

My hands are in fists at my sides, and when I come to Lincoln, I shoulder right past him. I can't look at him right now because I can't contain the tears anymore streaming down my face. I run outside and into the cold night air. I stand at the bottom of the steps, waiting for the limo to pull up and take me away from this world. I try to inhale as much air as I can, but my chest is constricting it. I am sweating, and the tears won't stop.

"Baby, what the fuck happened in there?" I hear Lincoln behind me as he places his hand on my shoulder. I push him off.

"Get the fuck off me, Lincoln." He grabs ahold of my arms and turns me toward him, commanding my full attention.

"Allie! What the fuck happened? Did someone say something to you? Who was it?" I frown at his assumptions.

"What do you mean, Lincoln? Why? Is there something I should know?"

He releases me and strokes his hands through his hair. Now that he has done that, his hair falls out of its neatly slicked-back appearance and starts to resemble the Lincoln I know. He takes a deep breath and motions for us to get in the limo that just pulled up.

"Come on. Let's go home."

I almost told him that it was not my home, but I bit my tongue. I don't know how to feel. I was feeling something for Lincoln but didn't know if it was love. I have never felt love before, so I'm not sure how it's supposed to feel. I just knew it was something special, and a part of me wanted to hear him out.

We drive back in silence, and once we enter the quiet house, I remove my heels and throw them to the side. I just want to go upstairs, slip into a hot bath, and wash all this shit off my face and body. I rush up to the bedroom and slam the door. Before it closes, Lincoln grabs it and pushes it back open.

"Look, Allie, can we fucking talk about this now?"

"I don't know what the fuck you are doing with me, Lincoln, but whatever the fuck it is, it ends now. I am going to get cleaned, get dressed, and then I am leaving this fucking mad house for good." I stumbled to the bathroom. Shit, I guess that last glass is hitting me now.

"Allie. Let me explain."

I try to get out of my dress, but it's fucking impossible. I can't reach the tie in the back, no matter how I push and pull my arms around my torso. "God damn it! I hate fucking dresses! I hate dressing up, I hate looking pretty, I hate pretending to be something that I'm not!" I scream.

I feel his strong arms around me and let the tears flow. I am so tired of trying to be something I am not. I cry into Lincoln's expensive suit and rub my makeup all over it.

Lincoln chuckles and pulls my head up. "Are you doing what I think you are doing?"

I look up at him, and I know I look like shit. I feel like shit. I feel like the trash they all think I am.

God damn, this girl can do no wrong. Allie looks up at me with those vibrant green eyes, and the tears flowing from them fuck me up. The mascara has run down her cheeks, and I just want to go back to fucking my girl. This argument is complete nonsense.

I have a pretty solid guess that the bitch Katherine told Allie. I saw her talking with her at the bar, and I will handle her later. I fucking hate Katherine, and now I have the perfect excuse to pay her a proper visit.

Kathrine has gotten into Allie's head and told her that she doesn't belong and that shit won't fucking fly. I know I need to be honest with her about this fucked up proposal. I was never going to marry Katherine, but my father wouldn't listen. He never fucking listens.

"Tell me about Katherine," Allie asks me quietly.

I hold onto Allie because I never want to let her go. She is my everything.

I take a deep breath and start. "Ok. My father told me when I was 18 that I would be marrying Katherine Sinclair when I turned 20." Allie blinks, and tears fall down her face.

Fuck me, her beauty is unattainable. She tries to push herself away from me, but I tighten my hold. I don't want to let her go. "I was never going to marry her. I told my father many times, but he never listened. Tonight, he wanted me to consent to marrying her in front of her father. That is why he texted me, and that is why we left right after." I held her closer to me waiting for her patiently to respond.

"What if he makes you marry her?" she asks me. I see the fear in her beautiful eyes.

"Baby, he won't. I promise." God, I love her. No one will keep me from her.

"How can you promise me something like that?"

"Because if he threatens me, then I will kill him." I shrug. Her eyes widen, and I wipe her tears away with my thumbs. The black smears across her cheeks, and now my dick is hard. He is ready for this shit to be over so we can move the fuck on.

I kiss her nose and ask, "So, can we get back to the main point of the entire evening now? Remember I said I was going to ruin you?"

She eyes me for a minute and then smirks. She's back. Her guard has been let down for me.

"Only if you can help get me out of this damn dress. Lincoln, please take it off me," she whimpers.

I let her go and rip the damn thing from her body. She stands there in the middle of the bathroom, completely naked. Just how I love her to be.

"Lincoln!" she protests. "That was so expensive!!" She looks completely surprised by me.

Damn this girl.

She has seen me torture a man for her benefit, yet she gets upset that I ripped her dress. She is more like my world than she knows.

"I will buy you a new one." I shrug. "Besides, you are priceless." I swing my arms around her waist, and she throws her arms over my neck. She laughs out loud, "Oh my god, Lincoln, that was cheesier than the one before."

I lean in and kiss her while I grab ahold of her bare ass pulling her against my hard cock. She moans into my mouth as I devour her tongue. I take one hand and fist her pretty hair. I pulled it so far back that she must strain her neck up. She whimpers again but in pain. And I know she fucking loves it. I look down at her and lick up the side of her face.

I take my free hand and smack her ass. Then I smack her tit. She moans, and I can tell she wants to touch me, but she waits for my command. She knows this game we play and how I want her to be.

"Please, Lincoln. Let me touch you now." I lean down and give her a gentle kiss on the mouth.

"Undress me." I stare into her dark green eyes and quickly drop my hands from her body. I take two steps back from her. I cup my hand and motion for her to come to me.

She slowly walks up to me. Her blonde hair hangs down now, and the hair around her face is dark. The roots have grown out even more, and I can't wait to see her darkness.

Fuck.

The collar I placed on her neck earlier tonight shines a vibrant green like her eyes. I suppose the more conventional term is necklace.

But it's a fucking collar.

She is mine to own and cherish.

I watch Allie come to me completely naked, never breaking eye contact. She puts her small, soft hands on my jacket and pushes it off my shoulders and down my arms. She undoes my tie and slides the fucker out as slow as molasses. The sound of the two fabrics rubbing together has me almost coming in my fucking pants. She bites her lower lip and rubs her thighs together.

She works on my dress shirt and starts at the top button. My girl undoes each one of my buttons at her leisure. My dick strains against the barriers that separate us. I am fucking dying here.

She pushes the shirt off my shoulders and down my arms. I feel the smoothness of the Armani suit as it leaves my body. Her hands run up my arms and down my chest. I fucking shiver from her touch.

What the fuck?

Shivering?

I suddenly can't catch my breath, and I panic. I don't understand the feelings happening in my body, but once I catch her gaze, the tension fades.

Allie's eyes speak to me, and I can't fucking take it anymore.

"Alright, enough of this shit. Come here, baby." I pick her up by the thighs and spin us around towards the bed.

Allie laughs so hard. "I knew you wouldn't be able to control yourself," she squeals.

"Fuck that, baby. That's not how we play. You know you like me dominating you and taking what I want." She smiles at me, and I hold her for a beat. Then, I plop her down on the bed and tell her to spread her legs.

And she does.

"Touch yourself, Allie."

She takes her hand and slowly grabs her left breast, twisting and pulling on her nipple. I undo my belt and pull it out of the loops. It makes a similar sound to the tie being pulled from my body. But the leather in my hands gives me a very good idea.

I lay it down on the bed next to Allie as I take the rest of my clothes off and throw them on the floor. Her legs are wide open as she takes her hand and rubs her folds. I can see how wet she is as she pumps two fingers in and out of sweet cunt. She watches my eyes, and every time I catch hers with mine, she pushes her fingers in more aggressively.

Her pumps are becoming more erratic and messier as she approaches her climax. I climb on the bed and sit back on my knees between her thighs. As I see her get closer, I smack her tit, and she comes hard.

God, she is a fucking goddess.

I grab my belt and tell her to turn over. She does after a few moments since she is still coming down from her high. I tell her to put her hands behind her back. I take my black Italian leather belt and wrap it around her wrists. Once I am satisfied, I smack her ass.

"That's my beautiful girl."

She moans, and I stroke my hard cock.

God, I can't get enough of her. I need to own all of her.

I slide my right hand up her inner folds and plunge two fingers in. She rides my hand like a fucking rodeo star, and I let her come again. Then, I take her juices and run them up her puckered ass hole. As if I stabbed a knife into her side, Allie jumps from me, trying to wiggle away as quickly as she can.

"Whoa, whoa, baby. What's wrong?" I move to her, but she is screaming and trying to get away. I grab her and turn her over in my arms.

"No, no, please, Lincoln, I can't do that...please, you don't understand...please don't make me," she cries and tries to wiggle out of my arms again.

"Baby, I won't."

What the fuck just happened?

I rub my hand up and down her face and kiss her gently till she trusts me enough to let her guard back down. I undo my belt from behind her back. She pulls her arms around my neck and pulls me into her body. I move to lay up against the headboard and pull Allie into my side. She is shivering so I grab the large duvet and cover her body and mine. I need to find out what the fuck just happened, though. If someone did something to her, I will find out, and that man is fucking dead.

I can feel Allie's heart rate start to slow back down to a normal rhythm. I keep holding her close and rub designs on her back with my fingers. Her head is lying on my chest, and I can smell her vanilla hair.

"Do you feel that?" Allie asks me so softly I almost don't catch it. Then she turns her head to look up at me.

God, I fucking love those green eyes. "Feel what, baby?"

"Love?" she whispers to me with tears welling up in the corners of her eyes.

If I had a heart, it would stop.

"Is that what that feeling is I have for you? I've never felt it before, really, so I don't know what it is."

Fuck me.

This fucking girl is killing me.

I caress her face. "I knew the first time I met you that you were it for me, Allie. I will always protect you, and I will never leave you. Now, I never knew the feeling of love either. But I can tell you this. What I feel for you, I have never felt for anyone else. And I never want to be without that feeling. So, if you are asking me if what we have is love? Then I would have to tell you that yes. This is fucking love."

She stares at me for a minute, and then I hear one of my most favorite sounds: she fucking giggles. "Wow, did I just hear Lincoln Reynolds III confess his love for me? I must be dreaming. Please, pinch me here." She lifts her arm that was around my torso.

I smiled and started to tickle her. She's back. But I can't help thinking about what the fuck just happened. Allie is a great manipulator when she wants to be, either consciously or subconsciously. I must be steps ahead of her.

I stop tickling her and wait for her laughter to fade completely. She lays below me as I hover over her. I lean down to rest on my forearms and ask, "Tell me what happened."

It's not a question but a command.

She looks confused for a moment, and then she closes her eyes. "It's a long story. I don't want to ruin the night we were having."

"Ha! If any night is to get out all our dark shit, I think tonight is the night, baby. Between my father being a dick, you discovering my arranged marriage and figuring out we are in love. I mean, come on, let's bring it all out tonight."

I moved off her and lay down next to her. I cover her naked body and settle in with my arm behind her head.

"It was just an old boyfriend of my mom's." I stiffen and breathe calmly. "It's trauma that I am still dealing with, but it's all over now. He was just a pedophile asshole who took advantage of me when I was young. I told my mom, but she blamed me for it and said I encouraged it."

I will murder a fucking village's worth of people.

I trace my hand up and down Allie's arm to provide comfort, but inside, I have a fucking wildfire spreading across dry land like an arson loving motherfucker. I need to get with Derek and find out every fucker who her mom has been with and find out who this dead motherfucker is. Her mom doesn't deserve to live either, but I will keep her around for now. She's on the growing list.

Allie clears her throat.

"What was his name, baby?" I ask, using all my strength to remain fucking calm.

Allie sniffs and closes her eyes. "It doesn't matter now." She holds onto me a little tighter, keeping her head down on my chest. "It happened a long time ago."

Maybe if I can find out when this happened that will help narrow it down some. Although, worse case, I will just kill every motherfucker who has dated her mom. They fucked with what was mine in some way, so they all will die.

"I am sorry that happened to you, baby." I cradle her head and stroke her soft hair. "When did it happen?"

She exhales before saying, "Well, it started when I was 14, but he didn't fuck me till I turned 16."

Mother

Fucker

Is

Dead

I get up quickly from the bed. "Where are you going?" Allie mumbles.

"I need to go handle something. I will be right back." I go to grab my phone already looking for Derek's number.

"Lincoln, please don't go." My fucking chest aches when she whispers to me from behind my back. I take a deep breath and turn around. Allie sits up with her naked chest on display.

"Please, just stay with me," her pleading eyes call me back to bed.

God damn.

I never thought I would see the day when a girl could stop me from doing anything I wanted to do. First time for everything, as they say.

I set my phone down and crawled back into bed. Allie turns over, giving her back to me so I can spoon up behind her. I bury my face in her sensitive neck and kiss her before she settles into my body. Her warm, soft touch has my dick begging for attention again, but I restrain myself. It was a long day and night. My baby needs sleep, and I need to wake up early to start searching for a dead motherfucker.

"Tell me something bad that happened to you, Lincoln? We can share our sob stories together," I hear Allie ask me sleepily.

I mentally sift through the bad memories that I have ever had. It doesn't take long to find the worst of all.

"Probably the day I found my mother dead."

Allie, who I thought had fallen asleep turns over to look at me. We share the same pillow now, and she looks like she might cry. "What?" she asks me softly while frowning. I take a deep breath and let it out while scanning her beautiful face.

"I was 8 when I found her. I had just been dropped off home from school that day when I came into the house. It was strangely quiet that day. We normally had someone working inside the house, but that day, it was empty."

Allie brings her hand up to pull some of my hair off my forehead. She rests her hands on the nape of my neck and starts to curl her fingers, running them up and down.

"I called for my mother, but there was no answer. I kept walking through each room until I finally came to her bedroom. When I opened the door, I saw her lying in bed." I see a tear fall from Allie's eyes. Her makeup is a disaster, but she is still the most stunning thing I have ever seen. I bring my hand up and wipe it up with my thumb. "At first, I thought she was just taking a nap. When I went to close the door that was when I noticed the empty pill bottle on the floor."

"Oh my god, Lincoln. I am so sorry." Allie moves her face closer to mine and kisses me.

I don't know what happened, but as soon as Allie and I confessed our darkest hours, something shifted in us. Our kiss had morphed from a gentle breeze into a hurricane. She grabbed my hair and pulled it so hard I moaned into her mouth. She knows we both need this. We need to forget the awful shit that has happened to us.

I didn't break our kiss, but I moved to lay between her legs. I felt her cunt, and it was ready for me like always. I lined my cock up to Allie's entrance. I thrusted into her without warning. She grunted and dug her nails into my back.

"Fuck, Allie. God, you feel so good." I tell her as I hold her head in my hands. I roll my hips in circular motions going in and out of her wet pussy. She arches her back and tries to take control from the bottom.

"Here, baby. You take the reins tonight." I slid out of her and lay on my back. I grab her hips and pull her to straddle me. Allie holds herself above me till she has the correct aim and then slams her body down on mine.

"Fuuuckk," I frown and groan.

"You like that, baby?" she asks me as she starts to ride me harder and faster. She chases her own orgasm, and I gladly give it to her. She fucking earned it.

"Take from me, Allie. Take whatever you want." I smack her ass and then grab her tits. I twist her nipples and feel her tighten around my cock. She stops grinding me once she climaxes, and I take the opportunity to roll her onto her back.

"Now, I will take what I want."

I fuck her hard and fast till she is screaming my name.

I fuck her so hard she will feel me for days.

I fuck her so hard that I ruin her for any other man.

I fuck her till she believes I fucking love her with everything I am.

Then, we come together. I pull out of her and roll her limp, heavy body next to me. We don't say anything more. We hold each other and enjoy the rush that lingers in our bodies.

I sit at my school desk, thinking about the evening I had with Lincoln. I should have told him about Carl and what happened to me. The incident happened so long ago, but it is still so fresh in my mind.

I was lying in bed with my covers over my face, hoping my mother wouldn't rat me out to Carl. I could hear them laughing out in the hallway. My mother was slurring more than usual, which told me she was more wasted than normal. I was worried about her even though she didn't believe me.

She must have been hurt by what my dad had done to her, and she just needed some help as well. Once I heard the bedroom door shut, I closed my eyes. Sleeping wouldn't have deterred Carl by any means, but I just couldn't stand to look at him.

I felt his weight on the bed, and I could smell his foul odor. He smelled like body odor and beer. I wanted to vomit.

"Hey there, pretty girl. Daddy is home. I heard about what you said. You think you can just tell whoever you want about us?" He grabbed the blanket I was using as a shield to hide my body.

"Please stop, Carl. I can't tonight. I'm on my period." I had never been happier to be on my period than tonight. But that wasn't what he was interested in. He grabbed my legs and pulled me down the bed so he could get on top of me. I was lying on my stomach.

He pushed my legs apart and ripped my sleep shorts from my small body. I cried and tried to get him off me, but he was too heavy. I heard his zipper, and then he spit on his dick.

"Tonight, I am taking something else from you, Allie. Tonight, your little ass is mine."

Then he shoved his dick into my asshole. I felt a heat there I had never experienced before. It felt like he was ripping me apart from the inside. He thrusted and thrusted inside of me and pulled on my head, telling me to relax. I was so sore, but he didn't care. He pushed in me so fast and hard that I bled once he pulled out of me.

"Damn, Allie...you got my dick bloody." That was the last thing he said to me before he got up off the bed, zipped up his pants, and left me there.

He left me there in blood, and I cried myself to sleep. I washed up the next morning and left for school. I never mentioned it to anyone till Lincoln. Not even Nick knew about what had happened. I was too afraid to tell anyone anything after that.

"Earth to Allie." I hear my name, and it pulls me from my nightmare. I look over and see Brittany staring at me with her heavy eye makeup and caked-on foundation.

"So, when is Lincoln throwing another party? I still get an invite, right?" She chops in her chewing gum and twirls her blonde hair.

"I will ask him tonight what we have planned for the weekend." Luckily, I was saved by the bell, so I got up and exited quickly. I ran outside to find Lincoln in his usual spot, waiting for me, leaning against the hood of his car.

"Hey, babe," he says as he pulls me in for a hug. I sink into his arms and inhale the smell of Lincoln. Cigarette and floral. It is a strange combination, but it suits him perfectly.

"Bye, Allie!" I heard my name. I moved my head up from where it had been buried in Lincoln's chest to witness, who called after me. Of course, Brittany. The look in her eye let me know she would still make my life hell after Lincoln dropped me, so to keep the peace, I went ahead and asked him.

I wave to her, saying bye while asking Lincoln about a party. He eyes me skeptically.

"You want to have a party?" He says as he grabs ahold of my hips, so I must look at him but unable to move.

"Yeah. Well, I mean, the only time I had ever been to one of your parties was when I was stabbing someone." He grunts and pulls me into a kiss. I don't normally give into public displays of affection, but my mind doesn't obey my body when it comes to Lincoln.

His kiss started out demanding but then turned soft. He lets me go and looks in my eyes. "Sure. I don't care if you want to have a party. Invite whoever you want, baby." Then he kisses my forehead and pats me on my ass to get moving.

I stand in front of the mirror and wonder if I should wear this tight red dress that I found in the closet. It looks expensive based on the number of stones that adorn it. It is low-cut and short. It doesn't leave much to the imagination.

"Fuck." I hear him say behind me.

"I don't know. Do you think it's too small?" I ask as I turn around to see Lincoln. He stands there in his black boots, dark blue denim jeans, and a black T-shirt. His hair is in its usual ruffled appearance.

He came up to me and grabbed my ass so painfully I could feel the bruises start to blossom. I moan into his hard chest as he picks me up. My legs go around him on autopilot.

"It's perfect so I can do this to you whenever I want to tonight." I feel his hands on my ass cheeks, and he squeezes them while he sticks his tongue in my mouth.

I throw my arms around his neck and pull him into me more. I rub my clit up against his denim, and he fists my hair.

"Fuck, baby." Lincoln breaks our kiss to look at my face. "You're so beautiful."

My heart sinks into my stomach like a boulder falling in a pool. I caress his face and look into his eyes, "You're not so bad yourself." I smile and give him a featherlight kiss on his mouth. "Now, put me down so I can finish getting ready."

Lincoln grunts again and then gives me an eye roll when I tell him my friends will be there soon. I tell him he needs to wait till I at least greet everyone before he takes me away.

I put on some black heels since I won't need to wear them for very long. I head downstairs after I put my hair in a high ponytail.

I asked Lincoln to host a party mainly for Brittany to get off my back, but I was super happy that Stephanie initially said she would come. I had promised her that neither Brett nor any of his teammates would be present tonight. Lincoln had promised me it would be a small get-together, and they were not on the list. However, right before I started to get ready Stephanie texted me that she didn't feel like coming. I knew she was still not comfortable being in social settings and I understood. I didn't even mention it to Nick who I haven't been in contact with since I moved in with Lincoln. I didn't want to see the hurt in his eyes or the judgement.

When I head downstairs, I notice a lot of people had already gotten there. I left my phone upstairs so that I didn't have to hold onto it. I also didn't have any pockets to put it in. I reach the landing and hear 'jealousy, jealousy' by Olivia Rodrigo playing on the stereo.

I do a once over the crowd and see Brittany has already found herself at the bar and is having shots with her minions. I see she looks perfect in her blue form-fitting dress with a small black jacket. She acts like she has been here a thousand times. She looks comfortable.

"Hey, you," Lincoln says as he comes up behind me. I feel his dick press into my ass as he leans his head down to kiss my neck. Tingles spread down my body from his lips to my toes.

"Oh my god, don't you ever stop? I swear your dick is never soft unless it's just come." I giggle.

Lincoln growls and bites on my shoulder. He grabs onto my hips even harder and pulls me into him. I start to think maybe this party was a horrible idea and fuck everyone else. Lincoln and I can just go and have our own fun. But then I heard her voice.

"Hey, Allie."

"Brittany," I say with disdain. I pat Lincoln's arm for him to look up.

"Lincoln, this is Brittany. She goes to my school. She was excited to be here tonight."

Lincoln looks up at her and then nods. "Cool. Have fun. Sorry, I got to steal Allie away for a minute. You understand." He doesn't give her a minute to respond. He just starts dragging me away with his hand in mine. I look over my shoulder to see Brittany fuming. I can't help the smile that comes on my face.

Fuck.

I shouldn't have done that. But hey, I mean, what did she really think was going to happen? I stop thinking about her as soon as Lincoln pushes me through a door. It's dark inside, but I still feel his hand in mine.

"Lincoln," I whisper.

"Yes, baby."

"Where are we."

"The library." He states it like it's the most reasonable thing to think of in a dark room, and then the lights come on. I am surrounded by a huge room with shelves that line each wall. They all go up to the ceiling and I see a ladder that is on rails.

What the fuck? As in, you climb to get more books?

I can't stop perusing all the titles, and when I look up, he is just staring at me. "Wait, how come I never knew this room was here?"

Lincoln shrugs and leans back on the dark wooded door we just entered from. "I was having some renovations done before I wanted to show it to you." His smirk gleams on his handsome face, and suddenly, I don't feel well.

My back starts to sweat, my breathing picks up, and I feel dizzy. I see a chair near me, and before I go to fall into it, I feel Lincoln's strong arms catch me. "Whoa. You ok?"

"Yeah," I get out. "I think I just got a little faint there for a second." I wipe my head with the back of my hand and close my eyes.

Lincoln places me on his lap when he falls into the chair I was heading for next to the door. There is a small table on the left of us with a Tiffany-inspired lamp. Everything here is expensive.

I don't belong here.

"Hey, baby, look at me." Lincoln cups my face. I stare into his blue eyes and blink a few times before smiling at him.

"I'm fine. I think I just need some water."

Lincoln picks me up just to lay me down on the leather couch across the room. He throws a fluffy, white blanket over me before he kisses my forehead. He leaves to get me some water. As soon as he shuts the door, I hear voices.

I got up and headed towards the door he had just exited, and I slowly opened it to get a view. I see Brittany talking with Lincoln.

There you go, Brit, served on a silver fucking platter.

What the fuck is up with this girl?

I can't even remember her name, but I know Allie pointed her out to me. I was heading to get Allie water when this bitch came barreling round the corner and ran right the fuck into me.

When she bumps into me, she rubs her tits up against my chest, so I step back to give her space. Sorry, sweetie, you're not my type.

"Oh, sorry, Link. I didn't see you there." She smiles and runs her tongue along her straw. She thinks she is being seductive, but she reeks of desperation.

I could give two fucks if she meant to run into me or not. Right now, all I care about is getting back to my girl. "Yeah, well, enjoy the party." I go to step around her, and this bitch cuts me off.

"Actually, I was wondering if you could give me a tour."

"Sorry. I don't give tours." I try to step around her again, but she grabs for my dick.

Fuck.

That.

I grab her wrist and twist it so hard she cries out. I pull it up behind her back and then press her body into the wall. She screams and cries when I take my free hand and then grab ahold of her neck.

"Listen, Allie seems to know you enough to introduce your sorry ass to me, so I am going to go easy on you. Don't fucking touch me ever again. You got it?" I pull on her arm tighter to make it twist more up her back. She yells out when I push off. I start to head back down towards the kitchen.

I make it two steps before I hear the bitch behind me. "It won't last. You and Allie." I look back at her over my shoulder. "She isn't cut out for this lifestyle." She lifts her hand up and throws it around to indicate the entire house.

I laughed and turned back around to head where I was going. She doesn't have a fucking clue what she is talking about. God, I can't believe I used to waste my time with shit like that. I have a fucking goddess waiting for me, and I can't wait to get back to her.

Allie

I have decided to leave Lincoln Hamilton Reynolds III.

He's fallen in love with me.

And that was never the plan.

I have fallen in love with him.

And now I must leave.

I have feelings that I shouldn't, and I will only end up getting hurt. I rub my fingers over my necklace and take a deep breath. As much as I don't want to, I must because he is ultimately better off without me.

After everything, I realize that I am not meant for him. I should leave so that he can be with someone who will benefit him. He needs to be with someone who was groomed for this. What was it that Brittany said? Oh yeah, 'lifestyle.'

Fucking bitch.

But she is right. I only hold him back. He should be with Katherine or Brittany. I am a nobody.

My mother never reached out to look for me or asked anyone about me, so I guess she assumed I left, or died, or went missing. Either way, she never came around. I am a nobody.

I finished closing out the bookstore and looked up to see Lincoln leaning up against the front door, typing on his phone. The street light glow mixed with the light from his phone gives him a looming effect. I admire him for one of the last times.

Stephanie still works occasionally, but things aren't the same. I don't live here anymore but I still like to be here. Finishing up at school has helped me make this decision to leave Lincoln and this city behind me. However, the biggest push came from Mr. Lincoln Reynolds Jr himself.

I was sitting in the theatre room waiting for Lincoln to come home. I was wearing Lincoln's black hoodie, some cotton sleep shorts, and fuzzy slippers. I had been messing with my necklace when I heard his voice.

"Allie!" my heart jumped, and I grabbed my chest. I looked over at the door to see Lincoln's father standing there in a 3-piece suit. "May I speak with you for a moment? Follow me." A question followed by a command: guess the apples don't fall far from the trees.

I swallowed what little saliva I had in my mouth and ascended off the couch. "Of course." my squeaky voice came out.

I followed Mr. Reynolds down the long hallway and down to the other level. We approached his office, and he opened the door. He ushered me inside and followed behind me. I looked around the dark room, seeing nothing but reference books lining the walls and a beautiful dark wooden desk. It looked just like the wood that made up Lincoln's bed.

Mr. Reynolds walked over to his desk and sat down. Even when he sat, I still felt like he demanded the room's attention.

"Please sit." He motioned to the nice brown leather chair across from him. I sat down and found my legs sliding before I knew I had been sweating. Great.

I cleared my throat, waiting for whatever this was, whatever he wanted me for. I sat straight up with my feet flat on the floor and my hands resting on my legs. I maintained eye contact and continued to wait.

He smiled as I said nothing but stared. "Hmm, I can see why he likes you." I frowned and tilted my head to the side. I wondered what the hell that meant.

"Anyways, I don't want to waste your time, Miss Parker."

"Allie."

"What?"

"You can call me Allie, Mr. Reynolds. May I call you Hamilton?" I questioned, knowing he went by his middle name.

His smile widened like a joker. "I can see why he really likes you."

Before I can rebut, he pushes off and comes around the desk to sit on it in front of me. He undoes the button on his jacket and lets it flare out around his slim figure. He lays his palms flat on his desk and looks down at me. "Let me cut the shit, Allie, and get right to it. Listen, I am here to make you a proposition."

"A proposition?" I inquire, wondering if Lincoln is aware of this.

"Yes. Look, I know you are not meant for this world, and honestly, my son is not meant for your world. They just aren't...cohesive." He pauses before saying that last word. His intention isn't lost on me. "Now, I also understand that my son has taken an uncharacteristic attraction towards you, and instead of trying to figure that out, I would rather just pay you off and send you on your way."

I am stunned. "Is this a trick?"

"I swear to you, Allie, this is not a trick. I want you out of my son's life for good, and I am willing to pay you off and start you out somewhere far away from here." My eyes widen, and I swallow. I am speechless as I try to figure out if this is real, a dream, or a nightmare. Not taking longer than a minute to think it over, he rushes out, "Do you accept?"

I didn't know what to say. Part of me wanted to shove the chair I was sitting in right up his ass. Part of me wanted to scratch his eyeballs out for being so fucking condescending. But the smart side of me took it at face value. He was offering me money and a new place to start fresh. It was exactly what I had been working towards my entire school career.

Three months ago, I would have jumped on this opportunity without a second thought. Now, I didn't know what to do because as soon as I was about to say yes, I saw those dark blue eyes looking at me. I felt those strong arms wrapped around me and those soft lips touching my body. But I couldn't say no; this was a once-in-a-lifetime opportunity.

I had to accept, so I did.

Hamilton said he had to make the arrangements so that I could leave without Lincoln knowing about it. Something about an assignment that Lincoln was scheduled to do. I don't know specifically the details, but I knew I would be gone tomorrow night.

All Hamilton promised me was that his son would be gone for the night, and I would be given a considerable amount of money to start over. He would also give me access to a private jet to fly out of town. Everything was ready to go except my heart.

I close the safe and turn off all the lights. I walk up front to stand with Lincoln as he pockets his phone. "Come on, baby, you hungry?" He unlocks the door and pushes out onto the street. I follow him out and try to memorize as much as I can because I know our time is limited. I try to keep my tears at bay while I navigate these waters.

"Sure," I say, not really feeling all that hungry, but maybe I will once my Xanax kicks in. Lincoln's father helped me get a prescription since he knew I would have to lie to Lincoln more once we decided to do this together. He even had the doctor provide me with enough refills to get me through the next few months. What a nice guy, right?

Just as I close the door to lock it up, Lincoln comes up behind me. He pushes his body up against me, and I groan from the force and feel of his body.

"Do you want food, or is your body hungry for something else?" He whispers in my ear. He drags his hands up the inside of my thighs. I get wet just from his voice in my ear and his hot breath on my neck. I closed my eyes so I could remember this moment.

His hands on my body.

His voice in my ear.

His hard dick rubbing up against my ass.

I would let him fuck me right here on the sidewalk if he wanted me to. I have no shame when it comes to him.

"Lincoln," I whine.

"Yes, baby." He kisses my collarbone.

"We should go home." He pulls his hand around to place it on my throat. He tilts my head back and kisses me gently. He grabs my boob, though, for good measure and slaps my ass.

"Fine." he huffs out in frustration but knows we can do more behind closed doors. So, he accepts my request.

I giggle and finish locking up. When I see that Lincoln has his back to me, I drop the store key behind the bush nearby so I can tell Stephanie once I am gone. I left a note for Mrs. Jackson, letting her know I left her in good hands, but I needed to leave the city. I apologized for not giving her proper notice, but that I had a family emergency.

When I walk up to the passenger side, I take a quick glance to look across the street. I just want to take a mental image of this place once more before I am gone. I blink a few times to register that Nick is standing across the street looking at me. He has his hands in his front pockets, and he's just staring my way. I don't know how to react, so I just ignore him. I am out of here soon enough and it's best if he just acted like I never existed.

When we get in the car, Lincoln turns on the stereo. 'Even Deeper' by NIN plays.

"Is everything alright?" Lincoln asks me and places his hand on mine. I look into his blue eyes staring back at me, and lie through my fucking teeth.

"Yeah, everything is fine." I look away and start to put on my seat belt, hoping that he doesn't see the tears I am keeping to myself.

"Allie...don't fuck with me." He states, with his voice dropping a lower octave.

I look back over at Lincoln and start to worry that maybe I can't do this. Maybe I should just tell him the truth, that I am not right for him, and that I should start somewhere new without him. I know he would convince me to stay, and it would only lead to heartbreak in the end.

I muster as much fakeness as I can and look him dead in the eyes, "Baby, just drive. Can we please get home already so we can fuck?" he chuckles and kisses the back of my hand. "Also, it's just that I am worried about tomorrow night." I turn towards him and run my hands through his dark hair, knowing it will be one of the last times. I look into his eyes and my heart starts to beat faster as I wonder if this is the right thing to do.

I push his hair off his beautiful forehead, and he leans in to rest against mine. "Baby, nothing is going to happen to me. Don't worry, your pretty little head about me, ok?" He nudges his nose with mine and I give him a flat smile.

"You promise?" I whisper as he leans over to kiss my lips.

"Baby, I promise. I love you. Nothing is going to happen."

My heart drops to the pit of my stomach, and I worry he will see the sadness in my eyes. But he doesn't because he turns toward the dark night and puts the car in first gear, taking us to his home.

"Come on. It's time." I hear Hamilton yell at me as I get out of the limo and walk toward the private plane he arranged for me. I have a small bag of clothes along with a new ID and an envelope full of cash from Hamilton.

I wore my Converse sneakers with shorts and Lincoln's hoodie. I couldn't leave it as much as I tried. My heart races in my chest, and I fear I may have a panic attack. I grasp onto my necklace and still wonder if what I am doing is the right thing. I love Lincoln, and I think he loves me, but we're just too different.

My past will always haunt me, and I can't get in the way of Lincoln's future.

I was able to speak with Stephanie before we came to the airport. Hamilton let me borrow his cell. I gave her my burner number and told her I would send her my address as soon as I got settled but that she had to make certain not to share it with anyone. She promised, and I left my old world behind. I told her to get in touch with Nick as well since I felt bad not giving him a goodbye. He deserved more from me, but I just had no more to give.

I climb the steps leading to the empty plane, fearful of my new destination. I don't know if my choice is the right one. All I do know is that it's the one I need to do right now.

Lincoln

Why it had to be this night, I have no fucking clue. My father told us it had to be done tonight with no questions and no exceptions. Shit doesn't feel right. It doesn't make any fucking sense, but here we are anyway.

The assignment we were handed over two months ago was to follow this poor schmuck. Obtain as much information on him as we could, search his house, and kill him. So that is what we did.

A fucking weak elementary assignment if you ask me. We could have done this job with our eyes closed, hands tied behind our backs, and gags in our mouths.

"Please...just take whatever you want and get out...please...I have a family..." the overweight, dark hairy gentleman pleads with us, thinking we give a fuck. I stand up from the desk and walk up to the poor bastard. I pull a cigarette from my pocket and light it up, flipping my zippo backdown and sliding it into my pocket.

"Sorry, Peter." I exhaled the toxins and cracked my neck from side to side. "We have families, too. It's just business. I know you understand." I slap his face and roll my finger in a circle implying for Tyler to wrap the plastic bag over Peter's head. He thrashes and shakes to try and breathe in the air his body so desperately needs but that he won't find.

I made eye contact with Tyler implying to release it. I love letting our victims think they may survive. It's the small glimmer of hope in their wide eyes that gets my dick hard.

Not as much as my girl does, but still, a hard-on is a hard-on after all.

Thinking of my girl has me wanting to wrap this shit up quickly. "Come on. Let's go." I throw my cigarette in the corner and Tyler puts the bag back over Peter's head. He wraps Peter's belt around his neck to fasten the bag in place and follows me out of the room.

Derek appears from down the hall with a bag full of shit. We wanted to make this look like a robbery that went bad. The fire we planned to set up came after the fact. We just thought burning shit would be fun, too, since it was such a cold night.

I grab ahold of my phone as we start to walk down the hall. I look to see if I have any new messages from Allie. I wasn't able to take her to work today because of this bullshit assignment. I open the message app and notice she hasn't texted me all day.

That shit is not like her.

My stomach drops, and I hurriedly call her number as I continue to walk out of this fucking house. Straight to V mail.

Why the fuck is her phone off?

"What the fuck?"

"What?" Derek questions as he and Tyler follow me out. I can smell the gasoline all over the house. Its smell is a breadcrumb path leading us right out the front door.

"It's Allie. Her phone is off. Fuck this…finish this up and call me when it's done." I slip the phone into my pocket. I jumped into my McLaren to head home.

"You got it, man." Derek walks over to his motorcycle and takes out the box of matches from the front pocket of his black leather jacket. I would normally stay to watch the finale, but the more I think about Allie, the more restless I get.

Allie hasn't been acting right for the past few weeks. I know something is going on, but I wanted to wait till she was ready to say whatever the fuck was on her mind.

Like a fucking insane person, I try her phone repeatedly, expecting a different fucking result every time.

I get home in record fucking time and throw the car in park. I leave it running because I don't want to waste another fucking minute without knowing where she is. I ran into the house.

"Allie!! Where are you?!"

Silence.

It's almost 1 AM, and I know the wait staff left hours ago. My father told me this morning that he would be leaving to go out of the country for business this afternoon.

I run up the stairs two steps at a time calling out Allie's name the entire time. I throw the door to our bedroom open so hard it crashes into the wall and swings back towards me.

If I had a heart, it would stop.

She's not here.

I search the whole fucking house, and every room I come to is fucking empty.

Where the fuck is she?

I tried her cell again. Motherfucker keeps going to voicemail. I turn on the locator to see if I can hear it ring out. I keep doing it as I walk quickly through each room. If she has been taken, then maybe it would leave clues for me.

I come upstairs and head down the hallway back to our bedroom. I can hear the locator noise getting louder as I walk further into the room. I hear a sound coming from the closet, and when I open the door, it's there on the floor in the middle of the room.

"What the fuck?!"

I pick up the phone, and before I throw it against the wall, I stop. Fuck, if Allie is missing, there could be information on this phone. I need to find her, and we are running out of time.

I pull out my phone and call Derek. "Hey man, you find her?" he answers.

"Allie is gone."

"What?!" Derek asks. "Wait, dude," I hear shuffling as he talks to Tyler.

I rushed outside and slid into my car. I need to find her. I will search this whole goddamn city until I find her.

"Wait, Link...hold up, man, what do you mean she's gone?"

"What the fuck do you think I mean Derek?" I yell into my hands-free. "I said she's gone. That means I can't fucking find her. Fuck, Derek!" I slam my hand into the steering wheel as I shift the car into 4th and then 5th, flying through my neighborhood. I keep a lookout around the road in case she is lying somewhere in a ditch or hiding.

Fuck!

I am going fucking crazy wondering where she is. Who is with her? What the fuck happened. My chest is pulsing up and down radically. I can barely catch my fucking breath.

Who the fuck would fuck with what is mine?

And just then, I have an epiphany.

That motherfucker.

"Ok...hold on, Link. Tyler and I are almost there. Just don't do anything till we get there, ok? Link?" Derek gets out in a rush.

Hitting ignore, I head down the street, and I know exactly where I am heading. I saw that fuck face watching us yesterday when I picked up Allie, so that motherfucker is my very first fucking stop.

He better know where she is, or he is dead.

I won't stop till he gives me something.

I wait in the dark with my hoodie pulled over my face.

Time is fucking precious.

As soon as his supervisor leaves, I wait by the loading dock entrance. I wait for him to come around, and then I grab him. I put his ass in a chokehold till he passes out on me. I go inside the boxing company he works at and pull up a chair to sit his ass in. I grab my bookbag that I keep in my car for special, unexpected occasions like tonight.

I knew exactly where he worked because I had Tyler investigate him months ago. I sit him up in the chair, and then I tie the rope around his body. I strap his legs down and arms so he can't move. His body is slumped forward.

We can't have that.

I smack his face to wake him the fuck up.

"Wake up, asshole!" I smacked him again. "I need some fucking answers."

He mumbles something incoherent, and I punch the fucker.

"What the fuck!" He yells out. I punch him again because I need to vent this frustration. I punch him because I love the crunch I hear every time my hand collides with his fucking face.

"Nick, motherfucker look at me!" I yelled in his face. "Where is she?"

"Look man...I swear to you, I know jack shit. She hasn't spoken to me in months...literally hasn't spoken to me in any way. No texts, no social comments, absolutely nothing." Nick exhales through his bloody face.

Fuck...

He makes me fucking sick.

I walk away before I murder him so I can think. I take a cigarette out and light it. I inhale and exhale with my eyes closed. I see *her* face cross my mind.

I need something to lead me to her.

The movement out of the corner of my eye has me taking pause with a quick glance. Derek and Tyler come up and lean on a few crates of boxes lined up against the wall. My boys knew where I was heading first.

"Look, Nick," I say with disdain as I inhale the smoke from my cancer stick between my blood-stained fingers. "I don't give a fuck if she has talked to you or not. What I'm asking you is if you know where she is. Those are two very different fucking things." I walk over and hover above his pathetic ass that sits bound in his chair.

"Also, did you think I wouldn't notice your little stalker tendencies yesterday? Come on, Nick...you gotta know me better than that. Why the fuck were you watching her?"

His chest moves up and down erratically as he tries to breathe through his busted nose. I circle him like a shark in the water. The smell of his blood churns the desire for me to kill.

I take the burning end of my cigarette and hold it just under his eye. "Have you ever seen someone get their eye burned out of its socket?" Nick cries and starts to whimper. "Neither have I, but you know what, I'm curious to what it looks like."

"Look...ok, ok, ok...let me see here."

"Ha!" I fake laugh. "Nice choice of words there, Nick." I emphasize the ick part.

He looks up from his chair that he is strapped to and squints. He is taking up too much precious fucking time. I tap his head and ask again, "Where the fuck is she? Come on, Nicky boy, give me something...otherwise, I will have to get creative with my tactics."

I motioned to Tyler to come to me. "Hey Tyler, hold Nick here so I can get creative."

Nick's eyes almost fall out of their sockets as he looks from me to Tyler. "Ok, ok..fuck...ok, I know who you can check with?" the emptiness in my chest starts to beat again. "I don't know where Allie is, but maybe Stephanie would know." Nick huffs out. His eye is starting to swell and turn a blueish purple.

"You mean the girl from the bookstore?" I question. "Why would she know?"

Nick starts to word vomit all over our shoes, giving us everything he knows about Stephanie. So now we have a lead.

We untie Nick, but not until I pull his head up by his hair and look him dead in the eyes, "If I don't find her in the next two days...I'm coming back, pretty boy, and it won't be pretty. You fucking feel me?" He nods in understanding. I drop his head and flick my cigarette against his temple. He crumbles in on himself like a roly-fucking-poly and falls to the ground.

"Fuck, man, no wonder she didn't give you the time of day. Now, you know not to fuck with what's mine." I kick him in the back for good fucking measure.

I nod at Tyler and Derek, who have been texting on his phone since we got here, looking for anything he could get off Allie's phone. But for now, we head out to Stephanie.

Allie

When I arrived in this new town, with only a small bag of clothes, I needed to find a job. I saw a sign in a bakery shop and stopped in. I met a red-headed girl with high-energy named Michelle. She was super sweet, and we talked for two hours. It turned out she needed a roommate and had a good feeling about me, so she offered it to me. She lived right across the street as well.

It seemed perfect.

I sent Stephanie my address so she knew how to contact me in case of an emergency only.

Michelle and I got along well. She had just turned 19 and had a small, petite frame. She told me she always had her hair in buns or braids and never wore the same outfit twice. Not that she had those many clothes, she would just switch them all up with different pairs of tights, or scarf, or earrings.

I was walking out of our apartment door when I ran into someone carrying a brown moving box.

"Oh, sorry…I didn't see you there." A young kid squeaks out.

"Hey, no worries, where are you heading?" I asked while fishing for my keys to lock up.

He drops the box and stands tall. "I just moved in. I live next door." He pulls out a yellow bandana from his back pocket and swipes it across his sweaty forehead. I look behind me to see the vacant apartment. That's funny. I don't remember that being available.

I put my hand out to greet him, and he didn't reciprocate. Okay. Maybe he has an issue with germs or touching. I pull my hand back, and he continues to lift the box he was carrying.

"Tony," he yells out behind his back as he walks on. He wears dirty jeans and a red T-shirt, and his tennis shoes have seen much better days. He reminds me of the boys who used to hang out around the trailer park back home. Thinking about home brings back memories of Lincoln and those blue eyes I miss so much.

"Rose." I yelled back as I watched Tony open the door down the hall and walk inside. I lock the door and head downstairs.

When I stepped outside, I saw the rain seemed to have stopped for today. A break in the clouds has the sun shining down, and the heat warms my body up. I feel like we have had rain for days, but then again, I think this city just gets it a lot.

I go to cross the street and wait because the pedestrian sign says to wait. Even if the streets are empty, I can't find it in me to cross. So, I get my phone out to wait till I hear the beeps. I figured I should probably text Michelle to let her know about the new neighbor.

Right as I am about to pull out the phone, I feel the hairs on the back of my neck stand on end. I get a chill that runs from my neck all the way down my spine.

Lincoln.

It's as if the air whispered his name to me as it blew past my ears. I turn around, thinking I will see him behind me. But there is no one there.

I close my eyes and try to slow my breathing down and inhale. Exhale. Count to 4. I close my eyes and take a deep breath.

BEEP!!

A car horn pulls me out of my fog and gets my attention. I clasp my chest.

Fuck, it's okay, Allie. Get a grip.

It's nothing; you are just freaking yourself out. I pull my purse up a little higher on my shoulder and cross the street. I walked into the bakery, prepared to get this shift started so I could get back home. It's nice to work in the back, so I don't have to worry so much about customers. I just like to blend in and not stand out. I need to go back to being invisible.

Lincoln

If I had a heart, it would cease beating at the first sight of her.

There she is.

There she fucking is.

It only took me two days to find her.

Two fucking days.

Two fucking days without her.

My Allie, *my* fucking Allie, crosses the street with dark brown hair, shorts that are way too fucking short, a white t-shirt, and black boots. She walks as if she doesn't have one fucking care in the world.

She looks void of any fucking pain.

As if being away from me doesn't eat her up inside so much that she can't fucking move.

Can't fucking breathe.

Can't fucking think.

Losing her damn ever-loving fucking sane mind.

That she would prefer the sweats and nausea that heroin withdrawals bring over the feeling of not being with me.

But no.

She is walking around like not a damn thing in life has changed for her.

My back breaks out in a sweat as I try to calm down the rage that builds inside of me. I drop further into my hoodie like she may see me behind these illegally tinted windows. Even now, she has this effect on me. I chew on my fucking thumb like a toddler. The bitch has been hurting since I've been biting the shit out of it for two fucking days.

She walks into the bakery she works at, and I can't stop thinking about what the fuck she thinks she is doing. How long does she think she can stay away from me? How long can I stay away from her?

The answer to that fucking question scares me more than I would ever admit. I slam my hand into the dash, "Fuck!" I can't fucking believe she left me.

"What do you want to do?" I hear Derek ask me from the driver's seat. Tyler clears his throat from the backseat. I take a deep inhale and try to think how I want to handle this. I run my hands down my face and close my eyes.

Think.

Think logically, Link. Don't let your emotions, or your hard dick, take over because you know you want to go in there, grab her defiant little ass caveman style while you slap said ass all the way home.

Home.

I open my eyes and look at the bakery. Wait a minute, how did she even get here? I never once thought about if she had any help to get all the way across the fucking country. Someone must have helped her. Someone back home.

It was easy to find out where she was. As soon as we found out Stephanie was 16 years old, we searched for the most likely place a secret would live. We didn't even need to talk with her directly. Like a fucking easter egg hunt, there the little slip of paper with her address on it was stashed in the back of Stephanie's diary. But I don't believe she would have the resources to help.

"You know what...let's sit on this. I want to find out everything about how she got here. What led up to this...what the fuck was she doing, and how she got here. Who was she talking with?" I look back at the storefront.

"Do you want me to stay back?" Tyler speaks from the back seat. I look through the store front window and see Allie getting her apron on to work. She smiles and shakes the hand of some guy.

That dumb motherfucker has no clue. He just made it to my list.

"Nah. It's all good. We have Tony in there now." He can keep us up to date. I give Derek a nod to leave this fucking town. My heart rate starts to slow as we drive further down the highway to the airport. I grab a smoke and light it up...inhale and exhale. I need to think this shit over.

But for now, I know she is alive. I know she is safe. I just need more information before I bring her little ass back.

Seeing her doesn't bring me relief from the restless nights I have had or the ache in my chest. Is she not losing her god damn mind right now? I can barely think or feel anything else. But suddenly, that feeling had morphed into something completely different. She chose to leave me.

Betrayal.

It bites like a son of a bitch. I have had friends betray me, and I have had family. But never have I felt this before. This is a bite that lingers, festers, swells, infects, and finally decays.

She had no fucking right to leave me.

I fucking own her.

Allie gave me something that I never felt before. She touched a piece of me that was buried so deep it never crossed my mind as a possibility for me to ever have. Not even my mother loved me enough. She took her life without saying goodbye or giving me any reason for her leaving. Now Allie does the same fucking thing to me. She knew what my mother did, and she still ran away.

She will learn a lesson that she will never forget.

She is mine and will be reminded.

I work on getting all the ingredients I need to prep for the day's recipes. Michelle calls my name to come up front. I walk out of the walk-in refrigerator and head towards the sound of 'Woman of the Hour' by Stela Cole blaring from the sound system.

"Geez, Michelle, might want to turn it down a bit, huh?" I smile.

Michelle just shrugs, wearing her purple overalls and motions to a boy standing next to her.

"This is Rose...she will show you the ropes back here. Hey Rose...come up front to meet our new stocker. Jacob...Rose, Rose...Jacob." Michelle says, motioning between the two of us.

I put my hand out to meet Jacob, and he gave me a firm shake. "Nice to meet you, Jacob."

"Likewise," he says with a genuine smile. He has dark hair but not the right shade. I shake my head thinking that.

"Well, come on back, and I will show you around the place." He politely follows, and I get my day going.

I end the day and walk back home. I am exhausted. It's been some day, and I am just trying to think about what my plans are for tomorrow. I climb the stairs and hear voices behind the door.

I turned the knob and walked in to find the new guy Tony and Michelle, sitting on the couch. "Oh, hey, Rose! Hey man...I killed you...that's not fair." I see the controllers in each of their hands and realize what is finally going on here.

Tony sits up straighter and watches me head into the kitchen. "Hi, Tony...nice to see you again."

"Yeah, same to you. I hope you don't mind; I met Michelle earlier, and she said I could come back and hang out for a bit."

"Oh yeah, that's no problem. You two have fun. Don't mind me. I'm just going to make something for dinner and then head to bed."

"Oh god, Rose...come on, hang out with us for a little bit," Michelle whines like a 6-year-old.

I know she means well, but I honestly just wanted to lay down. "Sorry, Michelle. I am just tired and would like to get a head start on tomorrow." I laid my bag on the counter.

"Oh yeah, what's tomorrow?" Tony asked out of nowhere.

"Umm, nothing." Nosey little person, isn't he? "I just have some stuff to do. Look, don't worry about it." I grabbed an apple and bottled water to throw in my bag. I headed down the hallway till I came to the bathroom. I lock the door behind me. I could hear Michelle apologizing for my abrupt behavior.

I pull open the medicine cabinet and get my bottle of blue pills to help me get through yet another night. I just need to relax and remember that everything will be ok. There is nothing to worry about, and Lincoln isn't missing me. I am sure he has already replaced me. I am sure Katherine has slithered her way into his warm bed.

I start the shower and get undressed while I wait for the water to heat up. The hot water cascades down my body and face. I close my eyes and see dark blue ones staring back at me. I rub my eyes with the palms of my hands and try to forget about him. I tell myself that what I felt was admiration for Lincoln and it wasn't love. We had never known that before, so how we we even know that was what we felt?

I hold myself with my arms and sink to the bottom of the tub. I turn the knob and plug the drain. I would rather sink in water than feel the dribbles wash down my body. Showers always fucking remind me of Lincoln. Just another reminder.

He's better off without me. I feel the warm water cocoon me and hold my breath as I sink. I turn the faucet off with my foot. I fell under the water until I felt the lack of oxygen burn in my lungs. I stay there till I feel like I can't hold it any longer, and then I stay there longer.

I scream out into the water, where no one can hear me, where I can scream as loud as I want because the pain is too much.

I sit up and gasp for air as the water splashes onto the floor. I inhale water and cough so much my chest squeezes. It hurts. I cry my eyes out and pull my legs into my body. Wondering why I allow myself to feel this pain. Why can I not forgive myself for the things I want and embrace them instead?

Why do I want someone to call me a good girl when I do bad things? Why do I crave attention from men who only want one thing from me? Why can't I get myself off? Why do I need someone to pull my hair or spit in my mouth?

I cringe and place my head in my hands. I fucked up yet again.

Lincoln

I feel a sting across my cheek and open my eyes to see Derek standing over me. "What the fuck are you doing, man?" I try to sit up from laying down on the couch in our Billard's room. This is my hell.

"Did you fucking hit me?"

"Well, you didn't move when I yelled your name, and I tried to shake you awake. What the fuck, Link? You smell and look like shit." He wears a backward hat, and his dirty blonde hair sticks out from the sides. I squint my eyes and look for another bottle of liquor to drink, but they all look fucking empty.

I rub my hand down my face, and my head feels like it got hit with a baseball bat. Derek opens the curtains, and my eyes feel like they are about to burn from the inside out.

"Fuck, man."

"Come on. It's been a week. I gave you a full week to drown your fucked up sorrows. Now we need to do work." Derek sits across from me and looks over me. "You need to take a shower, get some water, and we need to figure out how your girl got away."

I try to stand up and fall right back down. My head spins. I feel so fucking lost without her. My mind can't make up its fucking mind.

First, it was fear when I couldn't find her. Then relieved when I saw she was safe. Then fucking livid that she didn't care. Now I am drawing no leads on how she got away from me, and I need to know so she can learn a fucking lesson. If I don't know how she left, then I can't prevent her from doing it again.

But being without her is driving me mad. I just wanted to forget.

"Did you get anything off of her phone?" I try to swallow, but there's nothing in my mouth.

Derek exhales slowly. "Nothing."

I pick up an empty glass and throw it across the room. It shatters into a million pieces, and brown liquid slides down the wall. "She will pay for this, Derek. I don't fucking care about the reason she ran. I will make sure she never does this shit to me ever again." I glare up at him ensuring he knows exactly what the fuck I mean.

"I know. And we will." He eyes me with a look I have never seen on him before. He looks sincere, and for the first time, I see he understands my pain. "Look, we will find out who helped her, and we will make sure they know not to fuck with us. Ok, but you need to get yourself together because right now, we aren't getting anywhere. Your dad comes back tomorrow, and this place is a disaster." He looks around the room.

Besides the empty liquor bottles, there are dirty dishes all over the fucking place. I told the staff not to bother me because I just wanted to punch, kick, or kill something.

Derek's phone goes off, and he pulls it out of his pocket. I grab mine from the table and see it's dead.

Just like me.

"Come on, Link. Let's at least get you a shower. I will clean this shit up. And what the fuck are you listening to?"

"I told Alexa to play sad songs. She just started playing this." Freya Ridings 'Blackout' ends, and Derek tells Alexa to shut the fuck up. I laugh, and I think it's the first time I have since she left. It falls from my face quickly, but not before Derek catches it.

"Don't worry. We will find out who helped. Plan and execute some revenge. Then go get her crazy, betraying little ass." I sigh, knowing that what he says is the truth. I let him help carry me to the bathroom. He starts the water to get it hot, and I tell him to get the fuck out.

I finally can get into the shower, and I feel the hot water run down my face as I keep my head down. I watch the streams of water swirl as they fall through the holes, going into the dark depths of the drain. My darkness is ready to come out, play, and pull what it wants into its depths.

Allie will never want to leave me ever again once I am done with her.

And whoever fucked with me will be fucking sorry.

The pity party is officially over.

Ready or not, here I come, baby.

The first tip was when my father arrived back from his trip and immediately requested my presence in his office. He uncharacteristically wants to know how I am. He never cares how I am.

I sit across from him, wondering why the fuck he cares all of a sudden. "Alright." I shrug to see if he will lead my thirsty ass to water. He nods slowly and asks me, "How are things with Allie?"

"She left," I say, eyeing him suspiciously. His eyebrows fly up, "What, did you two break up?" As if he fucking would care.

"She just vanished on me. I came back from completing the assignment that you sent me on, and she was gone. No note, no message, nothing. Just gone." I keep my eyes on him.

"Well, son, you know, she was never really part of our world."

Bingo motherfucker.

He helped her. This fucking prick.

"Yeah. I should have known better, I guess." I take a deep breath. I try to think of anything I can to bring down the fire that is building inside of me.

"It's fine, son. But now we can focus back on Sinclair's. Have you been in touch with Katherine at all?" He opens his laptop and starts typing away. He is no longer interested in my girlfriend. He was able to check that one off his list for the day.

"No, I can't say that I have." I grab my phone out of my pocket and pretend I am texting her. "I'll reach out to her now."

"Good, son. This is a good thing. You will be happier with your choice." He glances up to meet my eyes, only for a second to smile, and then he is back to his prioritized task.

My choice.

I look at my father and think about what his neck would look like if I stabbed him with his pen. To see his blood sprawled out all over his important email, his laptop, or his custom Armani suit. I would see the look of shock in his eyes as he desperately tries to take his last gulp of air.

I stood up slowly and walked to the front of his desk. I grab one of the pens on the table and look back at my father. The instant before I decided to end his life, I felt the God of Wrath touch my shoulder and whisper into my ear, 'The taste of revenge is heavenly, but patience makes it sweeter.'

I stop. I drop the pen and exit the room. I head down the hallway while I call Derek. "Yeah?" he answers.

"We have our first name."

"Who?"

"My father."

It didn't take long at all for us to get into my dad's laptop to find out how he planned and executed his 'get rid of Allie plan.'

This motherfucker will die.

"Look, man, I know you want to get rid of your dad, but how the hell are we going to do that without getting caught? He is a fucking Senator." Derek says it to me like I don't fucking know that. I want to punch him in the throat.

"My dad must have enemies. We reach out to one of them and have a chat." I smile while taking a drag of my cigarette.

"A chat?" Derek eyes me for a moment, and then a deep grin spreads across his face.

"Let's look into who would be next up as Senator if something were to happen to my dad unexpectedly," I say the last word slowly for effect.

"Give me two days, and I will get a meeting set up." He grabs his helmet and secures it on his head. He starts the engine of his Ducati Superleggera V4 motorcycle and heads out of my driveway.

I am already starting to feel like my old self again. The faster I get this shit into motion, the faster I can get Allie.

I have been here for a total of 4 months, and I miss him so much. His hoodie no longer smells of him. Michelle washed it by accident one day, and I cried myself to sleep that night.

Fuck, that is a lie.

I cry myself to sleep every fucking night.

I had thought that maybe I made a mistake, but there was no way I could go back to Lincoln with my tail tucked. I am sure he has someone new.

Great.

Now, I am jealous of a hypothetical situation. I furrow my eyes together, thinking I need to stalk some social accounts.

"Earth to Rose…. can you hear me?" Michelle's sweet voice pulls me away.

"Sorry…I was just thinking about my application for college next semester." I lie as I fidget with my necklace while watching 'Unsolved Mysteries'.

"Oh god, girl, you are always worried about something. Don't you ever just let yourself relax and enjoy life?" Michelle said as she ran her fingers through her long hair. She was wearing it down tonight before she went on her blind date. "Speaking of enjoying life...what about you finding a special someone already? I know you get a lot of looks at the bakery...you should try to get on some." She looked over at me and winked with a grin on her face. She was putting in her earrings and getting her shoes strapped on.

"Yeah, I will get right on that." I giggle at her. I am not interested in anyone. Because I already gave my heart to someone, and it hurts too bad.

"I am serious, Rose. You need to forget about whoever this boyfriend was that got you so messed up. No one is worth that, I promise you." She grabs her bag and does a final look in the mirror. "Wish me luck," she yells as she heads out the door.

"Good luck!"

I stand up to head to my room for the night. I open my bedroom door and turn off the light. I fall onto my twin-sized bed and stare up at my ceiling. It's dark outside. You can see the lights flashing from the club across the street and hear the music faintly. I curl up into a ball on my side and wish again for the body I used to have cradling me. My protector. My lover.

This is for the best, I remind myself as the first tears fall.

And try not to think about my favorite shade of blue.

Lincoln

Tonight is the night.

Tonight, my girl comes home.

We wait and watch the girls come out of their apartment. Stumbling a bit as they cross the street heading to their Uber. My blood starts to boil as I look at what the fuck Allie is wearing.

Oh, tonight is the fucking night.

She wears a black dress that accentuates her beautiful body. My chest heaves, watching her get to their ride.

"You sure they are heading to this address?" Derek asks Tony.

"Yeah, man, that is it. I got it from Michelle earlier today." He exhales the smoke in his lungs as he tries to pass the joint to Tyler.

Tyler looks at the kid sitting next to him in the back seat like he would rather punch him. "Chill, man, it's just weed." the kid states.

"Ok, kid. Here you go." I threw a brown envelope full of cash over my shoulder. He delivered. He gave me daily and sometimes hourly reports and took a respectable number of photos, but most importantly, he knew not to touch what was mine.

"Damn, man, sure thing. You know, let me know if you ever need my services again in the future. You know, I even have some--"

Derek gets out and rounds the car to open the back before his bullshit continues. He pulls Tony out, closes the door, and gets back in to drive us out.

Knowing we are on our way to get Allie has my dick hard. My dick is straining in my jeans so badly I shift in my seat. We waited specifically for a night when she would be out and at a party. It's the perfect scenario to ambush and grab her ass before she can let anyone know. My girl will vanish for a second time, but this time, it won't be away from me.

We stand in the backyard of this fraternity party and try to blend in with the woods surrounding us. I haven't seen Allie. I need to get her alone before we can grab her.

I keep my hoodie low over my face and continue to look for her. A few drunk girls have come up to me and asked me for my name, but I tell them to 'fuck off.' They say some unkind things back to me. I ignore them.

I look to find Derek on the outer edge of the yard to my left. He allows some drunk girl to talk his ear off. He just nods and smiles as she laughs. His hoodie hides most of his face and he's dressed in all black.

Tyler, in the same attire, covers the right by just leaning up against the fence watching. He motions to me to look across the pool. When I do, my chest fucking aches.

I see her sitting on the edge of a lounge chair with that dumb motherfucker.

He leans into her as she laughs at something he said. He is too fucking close to her.

I am going to break his fucking nose.

Her hair falls in front of her face, and my dick twitches. This motherfucker raises his hand to push it back. Once he touches Allie, she flinches and pushes him away. He doesn't get the fucking hint and leans in for a kiss.

Fuck…

This.

I throw my hood back with every fucking intention of making my presence known.

I move from my position and start heading towards her. As if she felt me approaching, she jumped up from the seat and started running inside. I put two fingers between my mouth and whistle to get Derek's attention. I point toward the direction Allie went, and he heads out after her, disregarding the drunk girl.

Tyler follows me to collect Mr. Handsy. I come up to stand above him. He obviously had too much to drink. He buries his head in his hands as we approach. Tyler grabs this piece of shit by the collar and gets him in front of me.

"You don't know me, so I am going to give you a break here." I exhale, cracking my neck. "What you just did...can never happen again. In fact, you won't even see her again. But if by the very slim fucking chance you two do ever cross paths, I want it to be very fucking clear. You don't touch her. Do you understand?" I tap his sweaty forehead with the back of my hand. I wipe his disgusting filth on my jeans.

He looks up at me quizzically, "Who the hell do you think yoare?"

For fuck's sake.

I punched him in the nose and watched the blood shoot all over my t-shirt. I kicked him in the nuts. Tyler allowed him to fall hard on the concrete decking. I hear a few gasps around me from the crowd of drunks.

I pulled up my jeans enough to be able to crouch in front of this guy. He holds his bloody nose and cries like a baby.

"My nooosssee," he whines.

"It doesn't really matter who I am now, does it Fuck Face, hmm." I tap his head again. "Just know that you can't touch her. If you do...it won't be pretty." I slam his face down on the pool decking and stand up. I turned to Tyler and nodded. I looked up at the frat house and walked towards the door my girl ran through.

"Now it's time to get my girl." I headed inside, leaving Tyler behind. He goes to wait in the car with Derek, and I check my phone.

Derek: Top floor. Turn right. Last door on the left.

Ready or not, here I come, baby.

I wake up to an instant pain in the front of my skull. I try to lift my arm, but I see it tied to the bed. What the fuck?

I go to lift my other arm and feel that one, too, is tied down. I try to open my eyes and get my bearings. It's all dark except for a faint light coming from the left-hand side of me. I try to talk, but my mouth is so dry. I try to swallow, but I can't produce any saliva.

"Water," I get out softly and raspy. "Please…"

I hear boots walking towards me and see a tall figure approach. I can't keep my eyes open long enough to see but feel his weight when he sits on the bed next to me.

He lifts my head up from the back and I see he has a paper cup in his hands. He holds my head up so I can get a sip of water or whatever he has because I can't see shit. The water instantly covers my dry lips. I swallow and just keep going because it just feels so good in my mouth. It's a refreshing feeling having the wetness flow down my sore throat. I begin to choke, and the hand releases me. I fell back down on the bed with a heavy thud.

"Where am I?" I squeaked out. I take a big inhale, and that's when I smell him.

Floral.

Oh my god. It wasn't a dream.

I open my eyes and blink quickly to gain what little vision I can in the dark. Then, like a hazy dream, I see him. His dark features and deep blue eyes. He caresses my cheek, and I whimper.

"You have been a very bad girl, Allie."

"Linco--" he silences me by putting a finger over my lips.

"No, no, baby. I understand. It's ok. You don't need to explain." My chest rises up and down from my heavy breathing. I realize that I am naked, with only a thin sheet covering me. I can feel my necklace tickle my collarbone.

Lincoln eyes me and begins to pull back the sheet from my breasts. My nipples are protruding to the point of being painful. I cry when he gets to my pussy and feels my wetness.

"There you are. I knew you were still in there. My girl never disappoints. Of course...except when she wants to fucking leave me." His anger is clear as fucking day.

He slaps my pussy hard. I scream out loud from the sting that burns.

"Is that it, Allie? Hmm? Did you think you could run from me?" He slaps me again. His voice is calm and steady now.

I pull my legs up and try to move my thighs together to get friction. I am so ashamed, but I just need to feel it. I need to feel the pleasure I haven't felt in months.

"Awe, nah, we can't have that now. Bad girls don't get to come, Allie." Lincoln pulls my legs apart and straddles me, lifting my hips off the bed. He isn't wearing a shirt, but I feel his denim rub against my exposed thighs.

"You know, Allie. I have thought about all the things I could do to you when I got you back." He slides his warm hands up my thighs. I whine from the feel of his touch. "I don't know if you know this, but I have known where you were for quite some time now." He runs his fingers painfully slow up my folds. I feel my tears falling more freely now as I cry. My body stiffens under his control.

"You want to know what I thought about?" He leans down to hover over me now. His mouth inches from my own. I close my eyes, trying to gain some strength.

"Linc—" I try to get out, but he stops me before I can. He grabs my jawbone painfully and squeezes. I fear I am going to die tonight.

"Shh… it's ok. Don't worry…I am not going kill you, baby," as if he can read my mind. "I wouldn't do that. I mean, what purpose would that serve me…it doesn't make any fucking sense." He chuckles and runs his hands down my side, grabbing onto my hip bone. He squeezes till I feel his fingers dig into my skin. "But I do need to set an example. I need you to understand what you did to me, Allie. You took my trust from me, and I have never given anyone my trust."

His admission makes me cringe. I did this. I made him become this.

"Lincoln, please, I didn't mean it--" I manage to get out before he squeezes my cheeks even harder.

"You didn't what, Allie?" he says through clenched teeth. He leans down over my ear and whispers. "What? Tell me, baby. You didn't mean to hurt me? You didn't mean to make me feel something I have never felt before? Hmm, is that it?" he questions me.

I look up at him and try to get back to how we were. I know that he's still in there somewhere. I just need to get to him before he loses all that we had.

"Please, I was wrong...I was so wrong, Lincoln....please, I love you," he moves to my throat and takes my air.

"No Allie," he says and shakes his head from side to side. His hair falls into his eyes. "No. You don't get to say that anymore. You understand me? You never say that to me again. Do we understand each other?" His eyes stare into the deepest, darkest places of my soul.

I have no air to speak, so I nod to give him what he wants.

This is his world.

He owns me.

I blink, and he lets go of my neck. I cough so much that the burning in my throat intensifies. It feels like swallowing razor blades. I can feel the red marks starting to build from where my necklace dug into my soft skin.

"Fuck." Lincoln gets out in a rush. He leans down and kisses me hard. He bites my bottom lip till we both taste copper. He releases my lip and caresses my face with his large palm. "Sorry, baby. You have lessons you need to learn."

My eyes widen at his proclamation.

"Three, to be exact." He states calmly, getting off the bed. I feel the weight shift again as he removes his hard body. "And your first one starts now." He says to me as he walks out of the dark room.

He doesn't keep me waiting long before he comes back in, holding a little silver keychain. He climbs on the bed and pulls out a ball gag from his back pocket. He fastens it around my head.

I obey him.

He brings out a blindfold that he places over my eyes. I cannot see and cannot speak. He releases my hands with the key and swings my legs over the bed so I can stand. He then guides me out the door and down the long hallway.

I hear the slapping of my feet as they hit the hardwoods. I can hear the creaking of floorboards. The echoes I hear lead me to believe that I am in a large room...or house.

I smell flowers and instantly think of Lincoln's house. Oh god, did he bring me all the way back? Does his father know I am here?

My heart rate starts to increase, and my palms get sweaty. Lincoln places his hand on my shoulder signaling for me to stop. He drags his fingertips down my arms. Goosebumps rise all over my body. My nipples protrude painfully. My legs move on their own and pull together trying to gain friction.

Lincoln chuckles, and just like old times, my wetness pools. "You always did love my hands on you, didn't you, baby?" My 'yes' comes out, mumbled behind the ball gag. I feel the wet strings of my spit fall from my mouth.

Suddenly, my wrists are pulled upwards. I feel a cold metal wrap tightly around them. Handcuffs again and then he adds them to something above me.

Fuck.

He has me suspended in the air. I am standing on my tip toes to alleviate the pressure on my wrists. They fucking hurt. My arms are already straining, and we just fucking got here.

My punishment commences.

Lincoln

I have thought about this very scene for months now. What I would do to Allie once I finally got her back in my hands. Her fucking betraying little ass.

Seeing her now suspended in the dark and unable to speak, I am hard as a mother fucking rock. She moans and wiggles her little body over and over again. Wanting that touch that only I can give her.

Only fucking me.

She needs to learn, though.

I walk over to the dresser in my new playroom that was once my father's office. I felt it was poetic. After all, this was the place where the deal was made to send Allie on her way.

Not only is he a dick, but also a dumb motherfucker too. He didn't try to hide the emails between himself and his buddy, who loaned him their private jet for the night. He didn't cover up the fact that he had been having phone calls with Katherine's father about our proposal.

This cocky asshole thought he could get away with taking something more valuable to me than my own fucking name.

I open the drawer and pull out the black leather riding crop. I walk to stand in front of Allie. She is fucking beautiful, with saliva drooling from the gag and nipples hard as fucking pebbles.

She fucking loves this.

But she doesn't know what I have in store for her.

I grab a hold of one nipple and twist hard. She squirms at my touch and screams into the gag. My dick is aching so much that I release the top button of my jeans for some relief.

"I am sure by now you have figured out what this is. Right, Allie?" I whisper this last part into her ear. She moans incoherently and clenches her thighs together as she drops her head down. I grin, knowing that she is struggling right now. She needs my hands on her body.

I walk around her, dragging the leather crop over her exposed breast. She inhales, holding her breath for a moment. I slap her tit. She groans, and her head falls back. I see the red mark starting to populate on her round mound.

Fuck.

"Spread your legs," I demand.

She takes a few breaths before she does it. Once they are spread, I strap each ankle to the floor.

Now, she can't move.

She can't speak.

She can't see.

But she can hear my voice and feel my breath.

I can't take it anymore. I need to hear her screams and cry my name. I remove the ball gag and step back to revel in the view of my girl, completely helpless and at my motherfucking mercy.

Lincoln removes my gag, and I lick my wet lips. Relieved for the moment since I can breathe normally. The moment is fleeting, though, since I can't get any relief between my legs. I only feel the cool air flow across my exposed vagina every few moments.

I take a big inhale and exhale. The slap of the riding crop hits my nipple, and my body stiffens. The sting burns so fucking much. My clit throbs. God, that pain shoots straight to my pussy, and I clench.

Goddamn it.

I grunt from deep in my chest, hoping that I can express my frustration loud and clear. I feel Lincoln's hand cup my pussy. God, it feels so good to feel the warmth he possesses again. To have him touching me and rubbing my clit with his skillful thumb. He knows exactly what buttons to push and pull on me to get me where he wants me.

I feel his fingers enter me, and I can't help but crown. He feels it, too, and right as I am about to fall from that euphoric cliff, he retreats.

Fuck him! I groan, knowing full well now what my punishment will be.

Withholding my orgasms.

"Fuck you, asshole!" I spit at him. "You don't know shit, Lincoln!" I try to move my head from side to side to see if I can hear where he is now. Lincoln laughs loudly from behind me somewhere, but I can't figure out my surrounding very well. I am so sexually frustrated and tired from this game that my mind can't get clear.

"Oh, baby, that was just number one. I have a whole list of orgasms to withhold here before me."

"What?" I ask skeptically. What the fuck does he mean by a list?

"Yes, baby." I feel his hot breath on my cheek before he places a sweet kiss. I pulled my head away from him. "You have heard of an eye for an eye, right? Well, this is how I play that game. An orgasm withheld for every time someone touched you that wasn't me."

My mouth drops. I can't believe what he just said. "What the fuck are you talking about, Lincoln? I never touched anyone while I was away."

Smack!

"Ouch!" I scream.

Fuck...I feel the heat register on my ass and then feel his soft hand cup my ass cheek. The fire burning subsides from the cold, gentle touch of his hand. I push into it without thought.

"Fuck!" I exhale.

"That is not entirely correct, Allie. I have listed here the first time I saw you and him together. You shook his hand. Don't you remember?"

I try to think what he could be referring to. Who the fuck's hand did I shake?

Oh my god...wait, is he talking about Jacob?

"Lincoln...please, I wasn't interested in anyone else while I was away. I never forgot about you. I thought about you all the time. You must believe me, baby. Please." I beg. I can't see anything and barely hear anything over my own pulse, throbbing in my ears. I breathe heavily through the pain of my arms as they hang from above. I feel a warm breeze on my left side, and then I feel him.

His mouth is on my face, and his hand is on my throat. He squeezes, but not too much. "Is that right, baby...did you think about me?"

"Yes. I missed you." He tightens his hold on my throat. I struggle to breathe now. "Please let me touch you and show you how much I missed you." I'm able to mumble.

He releases my throat and kisses me once more on my cheek. He steps back, and I don't hear anything. The silence is deafening. I can only hear my heartbeat in my ears as the blood rushes through my veins. That is until I hear the buzzing sound of a vibrator go off.

Fuck.

I feel the vibrator touch my clit, and it doesn't stop until I am on the precipice again. Sweating and stiffening my arms, legs and neck, and I still get no release. Everything hurts. He wants me to feel only pain. He wants me to feel what he felt while I was gone.

He wants me to lose my fucking mind.

Lincoln continues to go through his list, reminding me of every time I hugged Jacob, gave him a high five, and patted him on the back until finally we reached the time when I last saw him by the pool.

By the end of my punishment, I can't feel my arms anymore. I can't feel my body anymore. My head hangs off to the side, and I can't move my legs. Lincoln comes up to take off my blindfold, and every time he touches me, I fucking quiver. I keep my eyes closed. I can't look at him.

I collapse into his arms once he sets me free from my restraints. I ignorantly think maybe I will be rewarded. But I am too tired to try. He carries me bridle-style back to our bedroom. I lean my head into his chest.

"I got you, baby. It's all over now. You did well. The first lesson is over."

Lincoln lays me down, and I sink into the cloud softness of his bed. He covers me up and gets in behind me. I feel his hand come over and rest on my belly. As soon as I feel his touch there, my legs push together. I whimper and notice how swollen my eyes must be from all the crying I did. My throat hurts from all the screaming I did…I cursed him many times over and over till I couldn't continue — till there was nothing left of my shattered soul.

He took it all from me.

That was what he wanted. He wanted to break me.

And he did.

He broke me.

Now, he will build me back up but the way he wants me to be. And I will gladly do it for him because I learned my lesson. I am his.

My eyes struggle to open, and my body screams in pain as I try to move. I lift my hand to my head and remember why I am so sore. My body was strained so tightly and for so long. I can barely move and every time I try to my clit stings.

I look over to where I see a glimmer of light coming from the nightstand. I found two pills with a glass of water. I don't know what they are, but I don't care. I take them and gulp down the water so fast that it spills down my chin. I feel drops land on my naked chest as I finish the tall glass. I put it back where I found it and lay down. My head itches so badly. I don't remember the last time I bathed.

I try to recall what day it is. How long has it been since Lincoln brought me back? I have no sense of time. The only indication I have is the light that shines through the glass windows across from me. As I peer out of them now, I notice it's black outside.

I slowly sit up, and that is when I see him sitting in the dark corner. Lincoln stands up and walks toward the edge of the bed.

My heart starts to beat faster. I pull the sheet further up on my naked body to protect myself. He strolls over to my side of the bed. His heavy boots are the only noise I hear besides the beating of my own heart thumping in my ears. I clutch my necklace out of habit and stare down at my lap. I can't make eye contact with him. I don't know how my body would react after what he just put it through.

Lincoln takes a strand of my brown hair and rubs it back and forth between his fingers. I wait quietly for him to speak. I hold back the tears as they threaten to come down.

"I knew this color would fucking ruin me."

I glance up at Lincoln's face curiously. His eyes never leave the strand of my dark brown hair that he holds.

"Time to get up, baby. We have somewhere to be." He releases my hair and heads to the door. He calls after me over his shoulder. "There are clothes for you in the closet. Dress comfortably." He opens the door and walks out. I hear the lock slide into place.

I let out a deep exhale. I got up from the bed and walked into the bathroom so I could brush my teeth. I think whatever pills I took are starting to make the ache in my legs feel better. I go into the closet and find everything just the way I left it. It's been months, but he never moved anything. I put on a pair of black leggings and a black oversized sweatshirt. I grabbed some socks and a pair of Converse shoes.

Knowing I can't leave on my free will, I sit in the chair that Lincoln was in before he left. I see he has a pack of cigarettes and a lighter on the side table. I never was one to smoke, but what the fuck do I have to lose now.

I grab one and start to light it when I hear the lock again. I pull out the death stick and put it down where I found it. Lincoln enters and walks over to me. I don't meet his eyes. He stands between my legs and then picks up the items he left on the table.

He tilts my chin up. I look at his handsome face and curse my body for wetting my pants. He wears his normal attire with a black hat on backward. I can see the dark brown hair pushed out on the sides.

"Come on, baby. Time for your second lesson." My eyes widen, and I start to speak, but before I can, he leans down and kisses me forcefully. He pulls the back of my neck up till I am standing in front of him. He never breaks his kiss. I can't breathe due to his assault on my lips.

I don't touch him even though I desperately want to. My body wants to grab ahold of his hair. I want to push and pull on him till he grabs me by the back of my thighs, rubs his hard cock against my center and allows me to feel something again. My body betrays me, and I moan into his kiss.

He chuckles and releases me. He grabs my wrist and pulls me out with him down the stairs and out to the black SUV that sits running. I see Derek in the driver's seat, typing on his phone. The light illuminates his grinning face.

Lincoln opens the back door and ushers me in. He slides in next to me.

"We're all set," Derek states and shifts the car into gear.

"Good," Lincoln replies.

I shift in my seat as I catch a glance at his tall frame leaning back into his seat. His legs are spread out, and his jeans have holes in the knees. He wears a plain black hoodie and dips into his pocket, fishing out a cigarette. He lights it while pushing down the window a crack. The smoke swirls and dances around his face and body as we drive off. He doesn't look at me or touch me while we drive.

I look out the window as the full moon shines down on the world around me. The silver glow lights up the city as we drive further away from town. I get nervous the farther we drive, wondering what he could have in store for me. Lincoln said he wouldn't kill me, but that doesn't mean he wouldn't hurt me.

I calm my beating heart by breathing in and out. That is until Derek decides to turn on the radio and play 'Nails' by Call Me Karizma. I catch his eyes in the rearview and see the grin on his face.

Asshole.

Lincoln

Derek pulls up and parks the car. The deserted construction site sits far off the highway. Our headlights shine, revealing a tall, unfinished parking lot structure. The site has several construction equipment all over so that anyone driving by would assume work was being done here but put currently on hold. What the public doesn't know is that this is one of the abandoned sites we leave for our purposes, for example, hiding a body.

I hop out and tell Allie to wait in the car. I flick my cigarette butt into the brown dirt below my feet. I walked over to the large hole Tyler dug up last week. He used one of the diggers left here. The hole is big enough to fit a small car. It's perfect.

Derek comes up beside me. "He just pulled up. He's bringing him around now." My dick gets hard with the anticipation of what is to come. This motherfucker thought he could outsmart me. He has no idea who he fucked with.

My eyes trail back to the car. I wonder if my girl is freaking out or has accepted her fate yet. She seems to be compliant enough, but after tonight, she will finally see not to fuck with me.

I see the lights of the G-Wagon come up and know it's Tyler.

About fucking time.

He parks the car on the other side of our makeshift grave. He climbs out of the front seat and goes to the back. He pulls out the man of the hour, who has a black hood over his head. His hands are tied behind his back, he's missing his jacket and tie. His white Armani button-down shirt is red. He stumbles as Tyler carries this asshole over to me.

Tyler comes to the edge and pushes the man to his knees. He removes the hood, revealing the gagged gentleman in front of me. The man's eyes widen as he takes in the scene we have in front of him.

"Hello, Father. Nice of you to join us."

If looks could kill, well, let's just say my job would be a whole lot easier but a lot less fun.

Of course, I am not talking about the looks I'm giving off. No, I am referring to the motherfucker who thought he was smarter than me.

"Go get her," I command Derek, without taking my eyes off my father. He trails off behind us. We are far enough away that Allie can see we have someone on their knees, but she can't tell it's my father. Hell, I wouldn't even recognize him at this point. I pulled out my black zippo and lit up the joint I had placed in my pocket. I want to savor and enjoy every fucking moment of this because this has been a long fucking time coming.

The incoherent mumbles I hear make my dick hard. My father's chest moves rapidly as his eyes bore holes into my head. I can't help the smile that forms on my face. I hear shuffling behind me as Derek brings Allie over for the show we have for her tonight.

And just like when we first met, I hear her before I see her. "Get the fuck off me, Derek! Let me go!" I hear the shuffling of feet as he brings her irate body closer to us. "If you think you can scare me or make me go down without a fight, you got another thing coming, mother-" her voice is cut off once Derek leads her to me.

My father looks at her with pleading eyes. Sad fucker thinks he can get her on his side to save himself.

Not a fucking chance.

Allie drops to the dirt ground below her feet. Her eyes remain glued on the hole in front of us. I stroll over and pull her chin up to look at me. The tears are starting to well in her eyes.

"This is your second lesson, my love. This is to show you what happens to anyone who may aid you in the future." She blinks, and two heavy tears cascade down her beautiful face. "He made you leave me. Now he will suffer."

I remove my hand, but her chin stays put. She's a statue of pure perfection. God damn, she is a sight to see. My dick twitches even more, but I am pulled out of my thoughts when I hear more muffled sounds and grunts. I turn around, take two more puffs of the joint, and throw it into the grave before me.

I look up to Tyler, "Take off his gag and throw him in."

I want to hear his voice.

I want to hear him beg.

I want to hear him cry like a baby.

The rip of the tape is loud but not as loud as the profanities that fall my way as my father tries to gain back some control.

He has none anymore. He sealed his fate the moment he helped Allie.

Tyler pushes him into the hole with a loud thud. My father tries to maneuver himself to stand, but he is no match for the deep, dirty hole.

"God damn it, Lincoln, you made your point. Now, get me the fuck out of this hole!" He yells at me from below.

I laugh hard and throw my head back. "Sorry, Dad. You made your bed so now you get to lay in it." I pause. "Actually, I guess you'll be buried alive in it." His eyes widen more. "But fuck it, all the same to me."

I nod my head to Tyler, indicating what I need for him to do next. He walks over to the cement truck and starts it up. The engine is so loud that I no longer hear the frantic pleas coming from my father.

"Sorry, Dad...After all, it's you who taught me to make sure everyone knows not to fuck with what's mine," I yell at him below before Tyler stirs the cement into motion. "I have to say, you did a fan-fucking-tastic job." I put my hands in my pockets. I'm eager to enjoy this show.

Tyler drives the truck to the edge and begins filling the hole. I watch while my father slowly sees the cement gathering around him like a grey pool. He moves all around, thinking he can find a space of security. He is screaming now, but no one will hear him way the fuck out here. That is specifically why we chose this place. There is a reason my grandfather wanted to go into construction. He wasn't a dumb motherfucker.

The cement grows higher and higher as my father tries again to get me to stop this 'madness.' Ha! The gray pool continued to surround him, and he was struggling against the weight. He is losing energy. The adrenaline is fading. My dick is getting harder, so much I had to adjust my stance.

"Lincoln…I did it for you, son. I was only trying to help you and your future. Don't you get it? We can work this out." His voice is strained from all the screaming.

"You know, Hamilton, if you had been a little bit more stealthier in hiding the fact that you got Allie out of my life, I may not have caught on so soon." I crouch down at the edge of the hole. "I mean, what the fuck? Emailing your friend to borrow his private jet and pushing so hard for us on our assignment. Tsk tsk tsk. I can't believe that we share the same fucking genes." I spit at his sorry ass into the almost filled hole. Fucking pathetic.

Once the hole is filled, the sounds have stopped. I nod to Tyler to head out. He gets back in the G-wagon and tears out of the lot.

"Go start the car, I'll bring Allie," I tell Derek.

"Good riddance, motherfucker." Derek says as he kicks a rock into the cemented hole. He turns to head back and I glance down at Allie.

I walk over to her body, which never once moved from where she fell. She never looked up from the grave.

She doesn't move; she doesn't speak; she doesn't try to run or scratch as I pull her up to me.

"There, there, baby. It's all over." I cradle her head towards my chest. I inhale the sweet smell of vanilla. "Come on. Let's get you home."

I'm ready for her third and final lesson.

Petrified...

Shocked...

Horrified...

Terrified...

These are all words that express how I feel now. The last thing I remember is the deafening silence that fell over us once the final layer of cement went into the hole and the truck was shut down.

I don't remember getting in the car, I don't remember getting in the house, and I don't remember how I got into this bathtub filled with hot water.

All I can think about is how Lincoln Hamilton Reynolds Jr. looked as he was buried alive in cement. The look in his eyes when he tried to plead for his life. Then, the look in his eyes when he knew it was all over... when that last layer of heavy cement solidified his life.

He was fucking buried alive in cement.

I lay in this large, claw foot tub inside this mansion and wonder how I got here. Not necessarily how I got into this tub, but how the hell did I, a girl from the trash, come to be here?

I am pulled from my thoughts when I see a dark, black shadow hover above me. I can't move, but I don't have to since Lincoln is here to carry me to my next destination. He kneels beside the tub and pushes the wet hair off my forehead.

"Hey, beautiful. You're going to turn into a raisin if we don't get you out soon. Come on, baby." He says to me softly and gently like he is worried he could upset me.

Ha! Like, I would do anything to piss him off right now.

He lets the water drain as he pulls me up to stand. He helps me out one step at a time and continues to dry me off with a soft white towel. I don't move unless instructed to do so. I don't talk unless I am asked a question.

He leads me out of the bathroom and into the bedroom that I now believe to be my cage. My knees hit the edge of the bed before he turns me around. He grabs my jaw gently with his hand and leans down to kiss me. His kiss is a soft, light feather of a kiss.

"This is your final lesson, baby. I made a mistake when I didn't claim you fully before. And I know that now."

What the fuck does that mean?

He pulls off his hoodie and t-shirt. He toes off his boots and removes his black belt. I maintain eye contact the entire time.

His jeans and socks land next to me. He stands naked in front of me, and my pussy clenches.

She is still a stupid fucking cunt.

"Lay down on your stomach. And put your hands behind your back. Cross your wrists."

I do as I am told.

I feel the leather tighten and try to adjust my back. He wrapped the belt around a couple of times to almost reach the point of cutting off my circulation. I feel the bed shift from his weight.

He grabs ahold of my hips. His fingers dig into my ass. I moan uncontrollably. His chuckle used to bring me joy, but now it brings tears to my eyes.

"I know, baby. You don't want to want it, but you can't help yourself." He cups my ass with his hands. "We can't stop this between us even if one of us wanted to, Allie. You were made for me, just as I was for you."

He pulls me so my knees are keeping my legs up to meet his. My neck is straining as I try to get into a more comfortable position. I feel his fingers touch my center and wince from the embarrassment. I am soaking wet and ready for him like always.

He pushes his fingers deep inside me and rubs my clit with his thumb. I can't help but push back into him as I chase my orgasm. He deprived me of so many the other night that I am too desperate to care anymore.

"Please, Lincoln," I beg because I have nothing to lose.

"Awe. Baby. Don't worry. I'll let you come." He increases his pace on my clit and pushes two fingers inside of me. That is all it takes, and I am finally getting some relief my body craves. With that, I let my orgasm consume me and fall off that cliff that sends me straight to hell. I paid for the ticket, I waited in line, and now I am heading straight to those dark, depraved pits.

I'm lightheaded and still coming back from my high when I feel his hands go to my back hole.

No...

No, he can't.

"Lincoln, please...please don't do this. I promise I will be good...I will be so good...I will never leave." My heart rate is increasing, I feel the beads of sweat on my forehead, and I pull on the restraints he put me in. He pulls my ass back towards him with his strong hands, and he digs into my pelvic bone.

My wrists ache as I try to turn them around to get loose, but nothing is working. My arms are straining to try and maneuver any way I can. He doesn't hear my words. He pushes into me with two fingers and spits to make more lube.

"This must be done, Allie. I own your mouth, I own your pussy, and now I will own your ass. Your body is mine."

I cry into the bed again, trying to get him to hear me. "Please...please don't do th--"

Lincoln cuts me off by grabbing a fistful of my hair and yanking me back. I cry out from the pain shooting through my back and scalp.

Lincoln slowly leans down and whispers into my ear. "Allie, we can do this the easy way or the hard way...I am allowing you that one simple kindness. I won't do it again." I take a deep breath and accept my destiny. Carl was never easy on me. He was pissed off when I told my mother about us. He pushed his small dick into my back hole with no lube except his spit and never built me up to it. If I allow Lincoln, maybe he will go easy on me.

"Ok...you win." I concede.

Lincoln

I drop her head down into the bed. She cries into the sheets. God, she is fucking perfect the way she looks right now. Her arms lay useless behind her back, and her wet hair is sprawled out all around her face. I have been wanting to take her ass ever since I met her. I tried to be a good guy. I tried to accept her wishes and leave that one thing for her because I knew how horrible it must have been for her.

But she fucked up.

She left me.

I was miserable for months while she was gone, and it never occurred to her to reach out to me. She never came to me.

I pull more natural lube from her tight cunt and rub it up and inside her ass hole. She attempts to squirm away from me, but I have an iron hold on her. She isn't going anywhere.

"God, Allie, your ass is so fucking hot." I slap it, and she cries out again. Just when I thought my dick couldn't get any harder, Allie proved me wrong.

Every.

Fucking.

Time.

I line up my cock to her puckered hole and start to push myself in. She is too fucking tight. I spit on my dick as it enters.

"Let me in, Allie. Come on, girl, I promise you'll like it…just ease up, baby." I feel her do as I say but not enough. She needs to relax and give in.

I lay down on top of her. I wrap my arm around her and start to flick her clit back and forth. She buries her head deeper into the mattress and moans my name.

Fuck.

I push into her more as I feel her release her hold on my cock. She moans into the bed, where her face is buried.

"Fuuuucckk, Allie."

She feels fucking amazing.

If this is what heaven feels like, sign me the fuck up.

I push a finger into her flooded pussy as I lean into her ear and whisper, "I won't hurt you, Allie, unless you make me, baby. Just relax."

She opens for me like a flower blooming on the first fucking day of Spring.

God. Damn.

With a little more thrusting, I get all the way in, and fuck me, does it feel fucking good. I sit back up on my knees to adjust my position. Her moans have become more labored now, and I can feel her letting go. My girl likes anal.

I smack her ass for good fucking measure, and then I do it again. I pound into her ass and smack over and over till I see a faint redness start to grow. I feel myself start to lose it in her like I always fucking do.

I lean on top of her and pull my hand around to grab onto her throat. I pull her head up so she is right beside me, and I squeeze. I can feel her throat muscles straining under my hand as I squeeze more. I lean my head into her neck.

I decide if she breathes.

I decide if she feels pain.

I decide if she feels pleasure.

"You are mine." I kiss the side of her face and lick up the tears that have fallen. I grunt as my body releases my seed into her. I thrust over and over till every fucking drop is inside of her. I let go of her throat. She gasps and coughs so much that it tightens around my flaccid dick.

I push my body off her once I can gather my bearings. Allie's body lays still as I unwrap the belt from her wrists. I see the red indents appear, and my dick twitches.

She lets her heavy arms fall to her sides. I drop the belt and pull her body up so I can lie down behind her. I don't want to clean her up at all because I want her to feel my semen exit her instead.

She moans lightly as I position myself around her. Her ass rubs up against me, and I feel her legs stiffen a bit before falling limp. She releases the hold she has on her body and sinks into me.

I pull the hair off the side of her face and her neck. I lean down and kiss up the side of her throat. I can see red marks forming on her neck from where my hands took her air away from those precious lungs, and my dick stirs. I pull her body against me tighter and nestle my nose in her hair.

"I fucking love you, Allie Parker. You are truly all mine now. I forgive you, baby." She tries to speak, but the only thing I hear is muffled sounds and a whimper.

She did good. She made it through her lessons, and now we can go back to the way things were before.

Allie

I am a shell.

I am a shell of my former self.

One could even describe me as a doll. Not just any doll, a sex doll for Lincoln Hamilton Reynolds III.

I no longer recognize myself anymore.

I go through the motions of daily activities. I get up, get dressed, and knock on the door to inform the guard who sits outside my room to let me out. I go to the kitchen, where Mrs. Fields makes me a nutritious breakfast. And then I head back to bed.

Sometimes, I go to the theater to watch the news. When Senator Reynolds went missing, I thought the police would come pounding on our door any day.

I mean, how can you just kill a Senator and get away with it?

I sat in front of the television that first week. I wondered if a missing person's report would be issued for a woman by the name of Rose Parker, but the nation was more concerned about finding Senator Reynolds.

That lasted for a week.

Someone new moved into the Senator's position, and suddenly, the news stations stopped reporting any updates. It was as if nothing had ever happened.

That was when I accepted the fact that I had no power, and he had it all.

For a while there, I thought I had imagined everything. Maybe I never left...maybe I have been here all along. Maybe this was hell. Either way, I stay here all day, every day, till Lincoln comes home.

I have no clue what he does every day, and I never ask. I don't say much to him. He tries to make conversation, but the old Allie is gone. The only sounds he gets from me are the sounds of my orgasms ripping through my body every time we fuck. He gets that out of me but nothing else.

I sit in the only chair that I have in this bedroom of mine and light up another cigarette. I decided to take up the nasty habit about a month ago. It makes me feel somewhat normal. I inhale the toxins and exhale, enjoying the buzz that only nicotine can provide.

I pull on the white frayed strings coming from the holes in my jeans where my knees are. I wear Lincoln's shirt. For some fucked up reason, I still love the way he smells.

I am fucked up.

I take my last drag when I hear the lock to my room click. I squish the filter into the ashtray and watch the smock circles die out.

"Hey, babe." I hear Lincoln call out from the door. I don't look up.

He walks over to me and grabs my hands into his large ones. He pulls me to a standing position and cups my face. He kisses me, and I open. I let his tongue play with mine in a choreographed dance that only he and I know. He grabs the back of my ass and pulls me in closer. I grab onto his neck.

He pulls me back and lets his forehead rest on mine.

He kisses my nose and whispers, "I have a surprise for you, my love."

I look into his blue eyes. My stomach drops. My mind starts to scatter with what it could be. I let him lead me out of the door. I have no other choice, honestly.

We travel down the stairs, past the kitchen, and into the backyard. I realize he's taking me to the basement where he held Brett. I suddenly can't swallow. My mouth is dry...oh my god. Who could it be? Could it be Stephanie? Nick? Michelle? Jacob?

I feel guilty for anyone who ever tried to befriend me. I feel sorry for anyone who wanted to help me.

We come to a door, but before we go in, Lincoln stares down at me. His blue eyes lock with mine as if he is looking for something hidden deep within me.

"I know, things have been hard these couple of months being back. I know you are not 'my Allie.' I hope this present will help you come back to me." He squeezes my hand once more before he opens the heavy door.

I walk in and see a man tied to a chair like before. Only this man I don't instantly recognize. This man is very overweight and balding. His head hangs low, so I can't make out his face.

"Wake up, mother fucker. It's time to die." Lincoln belts out.

This man's clothes are bloody. The room smells of piss and blood.

The man moans and tries to raise his head. His face is battered and bruised. But as soon as his eyes meet mine, my heart stops.

The one who abused me.

The one who took advantage of my young, naive age and groomed me to be his sex slave. He took away all my firsts.

He took them away from me before I even knew what it meant. He abused me.

"Surprise, baby." I hear Lincoln say from my right side. I look over and see a slight grin on his face.

Carl is my gift.

He is a gift to me from Lincoln.

Lincoln

I watch as Allie realizes who the fuck we have down here. Derek, Tyler, and I have been taking turns on fucking this motherfucker up for the past few days. He doesn't look good, but he didn't to begin with.

Allie looks to be in shock, but this time is different. I know my girl is in there somewhere. She just needed a little incentive to come back out and play with me.

And I knew this mother fucker would be the perfect thing.

When we started to research who the mystery man from Allie's past was, it wasn't too difficult. We questioned some of the neighbors and discovered Carl Waters was 'the boyfriend' Allie mentioned to me.

Lucky for us, Carl had gotten in trouble and was serving time in the local prison. Very fucking lucky for us, Derek's folks knew just the right people to pull us some strings. We got Carl out of prison on some bullshit technicality. The best was when we watched him leave prison only to be taken by us moments later. The fucker never saw us coming.

"There he is," I hear Derek say from the driver seat of the G-wagon while we wait for Mr. Carl Wilson to be released from prison, only to enter death row. This fuck face puts his brown bag under his arm as he approaches the car we have Tyler waiting in. We hot wired a random Toyota, made a makeshift Taxi sign, and hoped this dumb fuck would take the bait. I can't wait to wipe the fucking smile off his face as I watch him enter the black Corolla.

I flip my cigarette off my fingers and roll the window up. Derek starts up the engine, and we follow Tyler to the designated spot we have planned for this asshole. A whole fucking weekend at the cabin. I left Allie alone at home, sleeping. I can't wait to present her with him in two days. She hasn't been herself, and I know just the fucking thing she needs.

We follow Tyler but stay far enough away not to raise any suspicion. I doubt he is that fucking smart, but we cover our bases. Plus, we know exactly where Tyler is heading anyway.

We also supplied him with some alcohol, so this guy won't suspect a fucking thing when we jump him. I am taking no fucking chances — he will never hurt my girl ever again.

I know he is for Allie, but I get first fucking dibs.

We head out down the dirt road that leads to the small, logged cabin deep in the forest behind my house. Tyler swirves the car like we planned, acting like he blew a tire. He pulls over and gets out. We park behind him, and I pull my hood over my head. I put my fisted hands in my pockets and walk up. I doubt the fucker can see me approach since I am in all black, and the moon is hidden behind clouds.

I feel the devil on my side more than usual tonight.

I get out and walk up to Tyler, who leans on the back of the trunk, his hands in his pockets. Derek flips the lights on our car so it shines through the back of Tyler's. Fuck face looks behind his left shoulder when I open the right and grab the motherfucker from the back of his collar.

"What the fuck?!" he yells and starts to kick his legs.

The adrenaline in my body is surging, so I can easily shift the motherfucker where I want him.

I drag this fat fuck around to the back of the car and pull his buzzed ass up off the dirty ground. I turn him around and look him in the eyes before I knee him in the fucking gut. He hovers over, falls back down to the ground, and tries to catch his breath.

I kick his face with my steel-toed boot, and I hear the wonderful sound of crunching.

"Fuck, you broke my fucking teeth," he spits out.

"That's not all I'm going to break." I chuckled loudly into the night.

I let out a breath while I closed my eyes. Don't kill him. You keep him for Allie. Do it for her.

I look at Tyler and nudge my shoulder toward the bastard at our feet, who is still crying like a baby.

Fucking pathetic.

No wonder these fucking cowards pick on young girls who have no power.

Tyler takes Carl's hands and puts them behind his back while he pushes him down with his left knee. He puts the zip ties on and pulls so tightly I see blood beads form. The monster inside me growls at the color red.

"I'll meet you inside." I need to walk off some of this fury. I enter the cabin and go straight for the liquor cabinet. I take the McCallan out and pour a shot. I take one and then pour another.

Tyler enters, dragging Carl from his right foot. It's a sight to see this asshole try to squirm and squeal like a pig as his head hits every surface and leaves a bloody trail behind him.

Tyler knows we can't kill the asshole, but he's just as pissed at this guy as anyone would be.

Derek enters behind him and closes the door. He looks at me, and I take my shot.

Let's fucking roll.

We walked down to the basement and put Carl in the chair we had secured to the floor. Tyler ties his ankles to the chair and then wraps some rope around Carl's arms so he can't lift them up.

I take down my hood and look at this sorry bastard.

"Listen, I don't know what you think I have done...I didn't do it." He begs as his eyes are starting to swell.

I pull my hoodie and t-shirt off from behind my head. I walk over to the table of assorted torture items. Some are obvious choices such as cleaver, axe, saw, and hunting knife. But then we have some that are your common household goods like a spoon, scissors, or cigar cutter.

I pick up the dull razor blade and decide to start with this one.

"You don't know me. But you do know someone I care about. You knew her very well." My chest starts to roar to life, and a fire is stewing. I walk over to Carl and stand in front of him now.

"I'm going to take each one of your fingers here, Carl. And for shits and giggles, we are going to experiment on you." His eyes are wide as flying saucers. Sorry, Carl, not even aliens are coming to save your sorry ass.

Derek takes a small school desk and places it in front of Carl. Tyler takes a dirty rag he picked up off the floor and shoves it in his mouth. I turn and nod up towards Tyler, who takes Carl's right hand and slams it down flat on the desk we have in front of him. Derek comes over to grab ahold of Carl's neck so he can tighten and release on command. He is thrashing as much as he can, and spit flies from his mouth.

I take his thumb and start to cut into the flesh there with my dull razor blade. The damn thing needs to be sharpened. "Fuck, this is actually harder than it looks, Carl." I laugh as he is screaming now behind his gag.

The blade finally hits the bone, and my dick twitches. Fuck, yes. I try to saw it back and forth for a bit, but it's useless.

"Well, good. Now, we know razor blade is not a good fit." I throw the useless thing over my shoulder. Derek and Tyler release Carl for a moment to give them a break. "Thoughts on what we try next?"

Derek grins and says, "Cigar cutter. My money is on that one."

Tyler chimes in, "Dude, you know the axe has got to be the cleanest cut, though."

We took off all of Carl's fingers that evening, and it was fucking amazing. Allie can't tell now because his wrists are tied behind him. But nonetheless, my dick is hard thinking about it now.

"Allie," this sorry excuse for a human speaks to her. "Allie, oh, please, help me. Let me get out of here. Please you have...tell them I don't belong here. It's been so long...you are all grown up now, aren't you?"

This motherfucker...

"Shut the fuck up." I punch his face again, and he falls forward even more. His blood and drool mix falls from his mouth onto his dirty pants. Fucking disgusting.

He starts to whine like a baby, trying to get sympathy that he won't find here. I lean up against the steel table running along the side of the room. I place my hands down by my side and cross my ankles.

This room is particularly good for this type of crime because we have a drain in the middle. The floors descend so we can be as messy as we fucking want. And I plan on getting very fucking messy.

Allie finally moves from the place she had been standing in and walks around this fucking pedophile slowly. I feel her taking inventory of him and assessing her prey.

"Allie," he moans. "Please help me out. We can go from here and talk. There is so much I need to say to you...how I'm sor--"

Allie stops in front of him and laughs. I hadn't heard that sound since she first left me. My ears feel like they just heard Beethoven play Moonlight Sonata in person. It's the most beautiful fucking thing I ever heard.

My dick hardens as she continues to laugh so hard she cries. Her face has gotten its color back. It lightened up to that beautiful shade of red that I love. But this isn't my color, red of blood, or when I am deep inside of her. No, this is the color of fury.

My baby has finally come home. I push my hands into my front jeans pockets and sit back to watch the show.

Allie doesn't seem interested in hearing what this asshole has to say. She looks at me with joy in her eyes and asks, "Do you have a spider gag in here?"

Fuck.

Me.

"Of course, baby doll." I walk across the room to the cabinets and pull out what she needs. I hear grunting and more questions, but all of that is drowned out by my hard-on straining in my pants. God, I cannot wait to feel her again. The real her again.

I fasten it onto Carl for her so she can stay back and enjoy. Once I strap it on, his mouth is forced to lay open so he can't close it. He has trouble breathing through his busted nose as is.

It doesn't fucking matter. He won't be breathing for long.

Allie walks over to a drawer she is familiar with and pulls out her favorite knife. She walks back up to me. Her beautiful green eyes making me fucking weak. "Can you please pull his pants down for me?"

"Anything for you, love."

I pull them down as he tries to lift his hips. He is no competition for me. I punched him in the gut all the same. I wish I could kill this prick, but this is her kill.

His shriveled dick hangs out, and he leans over to where Allie stands. He still tries to look at her for sympathy.

My girl isn't stupid.

She stands in front of the asshole who took so much from her and grabs ahold of his limp cock.

She takes the jagged side of the knife and begins to saw off his dick.

The screams from him are poetic and just. His blood gushes out, spraying my girl and the floor at his feet. Allie finally gets his dick off, and then, to my utter shock and admiration, she shoves it deep down his throat. He gags on his own fucking dick.

God damn, and all that is unholy.

Allie stands back and watches as her tormentor thrashes in his bolted seat. It doesn't take long for his body to succumb, and he slumps forward.

I walk over to Allie and pull her out of her trance. When her eyes meet mine, I see her again like I did that first time. Her face is covered in blood.

"Lincoln," she whispers to me.

"Yes, baby," I whisper back.

"Fuck me," she asks and cups my face with her bloody hands.

Fuck.

Me.

Again.

And Again.

This girl is all mine now. That is all she has to say, and I am fucking on her. I devour her soft lips and pull her hair. She moans and closes her eyes.

I love how she has come back to me. She finally allows herself to feel what she wants and needs. I pull our shirts off and then remove her jeans. Allie undoes my belt and then pulls down my zipper. She puts her hands on my dick and I groan. I haven't felt her willing hands on me like this in so long. The thing in my chest starts to beat faster as I lay her down in fuck face's blood that litters the floor. I place myself between her legs and hover above her.

The blood has started to drain. It's formed puddles and streams around her head. Her dark hair is sprawled out, and her perky tits are begging for me to play with them. "Please Lincoln...I need you."

I put my hand in the blood by the drain. I rub it all over her naked body. My hand slides down her beautiful curves leaving behind blood red brushstrokes. Her body is a work of art that puts the fucking Sistine Chapel to shame. She moans and arches her back, begging me for the sweet release her growing arousal desires.

She runs her sharp nails up my back and down again. I hiss in pain. "Please, don't make me wait any longer."

And that, ladies and gentlemen, is all I need.

I like when she begs me to fuck her, but I fucking love it when she begs me to fuck her in my enemies' blood.

This is it.

This was the fantasy I had when I first met her. When I saw her and I knew I had to have her.

I knew then she was mine and would be forever.

I slam my hard dick into her sopping-wet pussy. I feel her walls closing in around me. She comes up to bite my neck as I fist her hair again.

Fuck, she is insatiable.

I groan, and she mimics me with her own satisfying noises. Her body starts to slip from the blood that has pooled beneath us. I held onto her shoulders to keep us in place.

"Fuuuck, Allie. God damn. I have fucking missed you, baby." I dive down to suck on her tit and bite her nipple hard. She screams out as the second or third orgasm comes crashing into her.

I can't hold on much longer.

"I want you to come, Lincoln. Please, come with me." I can't help the chuckle that escapes my throat.

Who thinks she has the power now? What's sadder to know is that she does.

I love this woman with everything I fucking am, and everything I fucking have. She is my dark angel sent to me from the devil himself.

I pound her harder and harder till neither of us can take it anymore, and we come together — just like my kitten wanted. I rest my forehead on hers and feel the light traces of her fingers on my back. I hover above her just enough that I can make out her beautiful face. It's covered in blood, and I have never seen anything more amazing in my entire life.

Whoever the fuck said fantasy is better than reality never had a sight like this in front of them.

I feel her hand come up to caress the side of my face as she whispers to me, "Did you know it all along?" I frown at her. "How did you know that we were meant for each other?" Her eyes scan my face.

I smile at her. "Because, baby, my soul recognized itself in yours."

She looks between both of my eyes before asking me, "Can I please say it to you?" she pleads with tears coming down her red face.

I pull the hair away from her face and smirk. "What do you want to say, baby?" knowing full well what she is asking me.

"I love you, Lincoln Reynolds." She smiles, and the emptiness in my chest catches on fire. I feel a warmth run from inside my chest and crash all through my body. It feels like I just had a thousand orgasms hit me all at once.

"I love you, Allie Parker." She giggles and pushes me off her. I get up and grab my shirt to pull it back over my head.

"I'm starving. Let's go get some food and celebrate." She stands and puts on the t-shirt she had been wearing before. Nothing else. Covered in blood and wearing my clothes.

Fucking gorgeous.

I get up tuck my semi-hard dick back into my pants. I take a deep breath. I inhale the carnage around me and exhale the sweet taste of victory.

I finally got my girl back, and I will kill any motherfucker who tries to take her from me.

The End

Epilogue

"Lincoln, stop," I tell him with a smile on my face as we spoon each other on the couch in the theater room. "Final Destination is starting."

"You can still watch it." He says to me while his hand dives below the waistband of my shorts. His mouth is kissing my neck, and his fingers have found my entrance. I open my legs up wider for him, wanting his touch on me. Needing his touch on me in any way I can get it. He goes in and out of me, and I can feel the wetness on my folds. I am soaked for him and only him.

His pace is perfect as if he knows exactly what my body always wants before I do.

"This is one of my favorite movies. Why won't you let me watch it?" I turn my face to look at him and pout, knowing how much he loves it when I do that. He grunts and then crashes his lips onto mine. I feel his hard dick rub up behind me, and I moan.

Lincoln pulls away from me and then moves to hover above me. "Who said I'm not letting you watch it?" He smiles and lands a gentle kiss on my lips.

I can't help but giggle, "You're distracting me."

He moves down to lay on his forearms and brings his hand to touch my necklace. "Now you know how I feel all the time."

He looks up in my eyes, and I feel at home. His blue eyes look at me, and I feel it. I feel the warmth from his body and the touch of his fingers on my face. I feel everything. I feel love.

I swallow and then lean my head up to catch his lips. We kiss softly and lovingly, but somewhere, it becomes feral, and we can't contain ourselves.

Alex Browning in Final Destination is exiting the plane on TV, as Lincoln decides he wants to taste me. He leans up on his knees and holds a breast in each hand. He massages them both and then squeezes them till I moan. He moves down further on my body and removes my satin sleep shorts. He kisses my thighs and bites for good measure, as he likes to call it. I giggle when he runs his wet tongue down to my center.

God, it feels so good.

"Let me worship you, Allie." And then he dives into my cunt. Granted I have been upset with her in the past, but when all was said and done, she led me here. She led me to Lincoln Hamilton Reynolds III, and I could not be any happier.

I feel his tongue expertly go in and out of my vagina, and then he sucks on my clit. His hands hang onto my legs keeping me where he wants me. I arch my back because I am so fucking close. Just a little bit longer and I will get my reward. I grab onto Lincoln's head and feel his soft brown hair run through my hands. I take a fistful of his locks and force him down where *I* want him. He chuckles but continues to lick and love my opening with every suck and kiss from his soft lips.

I used to think Lincoln had all the power. But I finally learned something. He may have immense power, but I hold the ultimate one in the palms of my small, filthy hands.

I hold his heart.

I hold his love.

I hold him.

I didn't think I was meant for this world, but it turns out I was fucking custom-made for it.

Thank You!

Thank you for reading my story and diving into the depths of Lincoln & Allie's love.

If you liked my book, the best way you can help an Indie publisher like me is to give a review on Amazon and/or Goodreads.

Email - melaniecrimauthor@gmail.com

Website - www.melaniecrimauthor.com

ACKNOWLEDGMENT

First and foremost, my family for their undying support. Without them, I would have never been able to fulfill my dream of being a published writer.

My sister, for being my number one fan.

My friends who encouraged me throughout this entire process.

My therapist, because we all go a little mad sometimes and we all need that calm voice in our corner.

ABOUT THE AUTHOR

Melanie lives in NC with her husband, two daughters, two rescue dogs, and one rescued cat. Her favorite holiday is Halloween, and she discovered Dark Romance in 2024. She was excited to see that others loved dark entertainment just as much as she did.